SCOT
MCC   N

THE COLLECTED WORKS
Volume 1

Foreword by
BLAKE BUTLER

Afterword by
SAM PINK

LAZY FASCIST PRESS

Praise for Scott McClanahan

"Scott McClanahan is a powerful, exceptional writer, and the overall effect of reading his deceptively simple stories is like getting hit in the head by a champion cage fighter cranked up on meth that was cooked in a trailer without running water in some Kentucky backwoods where people sing murder ballads to their children to put them to sleep."
—**DONALD RAY POLLOCK**, author of *The Devil All the Time*

"He might be one of the great southern storytellers of our time."
—**VOL. 1 BROOKLYN**

"When I discovered the stories of Scott McClanahan last year, I was instantly enthralled with his natural storytelling voice and freaky funny tales. There's no pretense to Scott's work. It's like you're just dropped right into the middle of these fantastic and true stories. It's like a sweet blend of my favorite southern writers, Larry Brown and Harry Crews. Reading McClanahan is like listening to a good friend telling you his best real-life stories on your back porch on a humid night. And you both got a nice whiskey buzz going."
—**KEVIN SAMPSELL**, author of A Common Pornography

"McClanahan's prose is unfettered and kinetic and his stories seem like a hyper-modern iteration of local color fiction. His delivery is guileless and his morality ambivalent and you get the sense, while reading him, that he is sitting next to you on a barstool, eating peanuts and drinking a beer, and intermittently getting up to pick a song on the jukebox."
—**THE RUMPUS**

"Reads like Bukowski with more surprises."
—**IMPOSE MAGAZINE**

"You'll encounter a hernia dog, a fight over a thrown bologna sandwich, and a man named Poop Deck Pappy, 'who goes to the wakes at Wallace and Wallace funeral home, even though he never

knew the people being waked.' You'll witness what the Prettiest Girl in Texas is hiding up her sleeve, watch a possum 'become the most beautiful star shooting across the dark dark sky,' and see a young boy dressed like a baby doll imagine himself 'a soldier in some far away land, searching for something beautiful to kill.' All stories are written naturally, in a conversational tone, as if taken in dictation from a narrator named Scott."
—INSIDE HIGHERED

"Scott McClanahan is holding your hand. Scott McClanahan is singing a spiritual, doing a jig, telling a story, and turning a can of tomato soup into a can of chicken soup. The condensed kind. He is showing you the story then turning it inside out and showing you that it is exactly the same thing on the inside, only moreso. On the inside of the black bear there are a lot more bits of black bear. Inside the sock is the interior sock and a bunch of rocks. Scott McClanahan put them there."
—THE FANZINE

"If you can't get Scott McClanahan to come tell you stories at your neighborhood bar, try just taking his book *Stories* and reading it aloud to friends. McClanahan's short stories are just that informal, and just that engaging."
—PITTSBURGH CITY PAPER

"Fuck, this guy's good."
—GIANCARLO DITRAPANO, editor of *New York Tyrant*

A Lazy Fascist Original

Lazy Fascist Press
An Imprint of Eraserhead Press
205 NE Bryant Street
Portland, Oregon 97211

www.lazyfascistpress.com

ISBN: 978-1-62105-033-9

TABLE OF CONTENTS

FOR SARAH

THE MAN WHO KILLED YOU

A Foreword by Blake Butler

Man comes into the small white room where you are sitting and tells you he has a gun. He is of medium height, nearly clean-shaven, wearing a seersucker suit that fits his shape. He has a look in his eyes like light is being strangled and he likes it, but you don't see any gun. You are seated on a small metal chair beside someone you used to remember, used to like or know in some way beyond just being, though now it doesn't seem like either of those are so much true. You had not meant to be here today. You feel as if you have been shrinking for several years. Before you can think any more about that or about the gun or what is coming through the windows framing the far wall, the man pulls out the gun and holds the gun up at you and shoots you in the face. The sound is loud and silent at the same time. It is over before it ends. You aren't there to see your blood hit the light and hit your flesh and hit your friend who was no longer such a friend as he had been. It splashes on the fine seersucker suit of the man before you who has shot you and whose expression has not changed, he is standing still in the white room with his skin there and he is raising up his hands, he is beginning to speak aloud in a voice that comes not from inside him but from almost on the air itself, the air with your blood inside it, where you had lived once. No one is moving in the room. Whoever's there, the name and number of bodies of which you will have no recollection, having seen this man now shoot you point blank in the face, they don't seem shocked or weird at all about it, they have not moved at all in how they stand, they are looking up straight ahead into the wide eyes of the man who killed you, from which the voice now raises in the room, moving through the space with rising volume in the air where you have died. The voice fills in along the space where there should have been someone in you there to hear and take the word, the word you'd heard on lips before but not like now all dead as fuck, in the voice of the man covered in your blood some as he moves forth and begins to vibrate slightly, in the sound around you filling space, in this room you had come today to walk around in and drink beer in and make small talk and touch hands, and now cannot because you are dead and you are being filled with sound, with the voice of the man who killed you and his voice is larger than the shot had been somehow and the sound is winding through your lungs, as if you, the dead one, are also speaking, though you can't remember already who you were, and in your voice are several hundred other voices you do not remember holding, you can't feel the fields where in you the word has stitched itself inside your space and legs and lungs, and yet it feels light, it feels like bloating open in a hole overflowing with white ash and whiter milk, and in the room around you everyone is raising up their arms to match the raised arms of the man who killed you, who is shouting, and they are shouting too though they don't move, the sound instead is winding all around them, and the man is grinning, or is he laughing, he spreads his fingers like a scout, he smells like fires lit years later, he's lifted slightly off the ground, his arms above him at the ceiling as if to touch something above the room where he has killed you, the gun now just ridges in his hand, the air where you are not and never had been but had tried to live and be a friend, and in your lungs the voice is wearing all your other voices, and in the dark you open wide and you stand up.

THE LAST TIME I SAW RANDY DOOGAN

The last time I saw Randy Doogan was just a couple of years ago. It all happened after I left home and was working as a telemarketer in Huntington. One day I went back home to visit my parents for the weekend and the phone rang. I went over to the phone and let it ring one more time like people always do, and then I picked it up.

"Hello," I said and there was this voice on the other end that sounded familiar.

"Hey Scott. This is Randy."

It had probably been ten years since I last heard this voice, and all that I'd heard about Randy for the past couple of years had been bad.

He was on methamphetamine.

He was married to a girl named Catfish.

He was divorced.

His life was falling apart.

It was strange too because he was always the cool guy in high school. He was the older guy who told us all about sex in the first grade. He was the crazy guy. He was the guy who quit the basketball team in the middle of a game so he could go have sex with this older woman he met in the gym that night. He was the guy who showed up the next day wearing her panties and walked around the locker room like there was nothing unusual about it. This was the guy whose brothers used to break into houses, get sent off to prison, and come back with stories about soap on the rope.

So I knew if he was having problems to be careful about talking to him.

I said, "Oh yeah. What's been going on?" in a voice that was already looking for a reason to get off the phone.

But Randy's voice just quivered all nervous and he finally said,

"Now I know we haven't talked in a long time, but I've just been having a real hard time lately."

I already thought, "Oh God, he wants to get some money off of me." That's exactly what he wanted all right, as he started in on how hard he had it and how this girl named Catfish had ruined his life. Then he said he wondered if my folks were still living where they used to live (I didn't tell him they moved because I didn't want them to get robbed). Before I could make up a lie to tell him, he went into how he completely understood if I didn't want to, but he needed to borrow fifty dollars.

I knew it.

So I started thinking up excuses of why I couldn't give it to him, of how I was broke, it's late, the bank wasn't open, you could probably find someone else, etc., etc. But then he told me the real reason why.

He told me, "I completely understand if you can't, but my brother James was killed in a car accident this morning. He was killed in a car accident in Delaware and I need the money to get up there and go to his wake."

I knew it was wrong of me, but inside my head I was still wondering if this was all a lie. I was wondering if he needed the money to get high and he was using it as an excuse. So I told him it was late (it was), and if he still needed the money to call me in the morning and I'd get it for him (I thought he would find someone else he could hit up for a fix).

But then…he called me up the next morning and said he still needed the money.

"I'm sorry Scott, but if you could I'd really appreciate it."

I knew he wasn't lying. I went down to the bank as soon as they opened, thinking "Scott you shouldn't be so damn judgmental. Here was somebody you've known since childhood and all he needs is a little help. I mean for fuck sake his brother was just killed."

So instead of getting him fifty dollars, I took out seventy-five. I figured if he was going to Delaware fifty dollars wouldn't get him much of anything. I met him down at Go-Mart because I still didn't want him to know where my parents lived. When I pulled in, he was waiting for me in the back of a rickety old car that was covered in rust spots and full of people. I stopped the car and walked over to them, and Randy squeezed out from behind the back seat. When I saw him I stopped because he looked so different than before. He had a pot belly now and skinny legs, and the wiry thirteen-year-old boy mustache, which made him look so much older in junior high just made him look dirty now. We shook hands and I couldn't get over how different he looked. I gave him the money.

And so, as he was just about ready to turn around and get back into the rickety old car, I said, "Randy?"

Randy stopped.

I stood there and wanted to say something that was memorable for him.

I wanted to say something that inspired him.

I wanted to say something about how I remembered when he wore that woman's panties and how funny it was.

I wanted to say something that made him think I was a real friend.

I wanted to explain how it was wrong that I doubted him.

My voice cracked and all I could say was, "You know what Randy? Your brother was the best of you Doogans."

Randy just looked at me like he was overwhelmed by my sentiment. There were tears in his eyes and he kept looking at the ground.

Then he said, " Yeah. He was a good brother. He was a real good brother."

Then it was quiet for a second and he said, "I better get going and take care of business. It's going to be a long drive."

I shook my head yes and watched him squeeze into the back of the car. Then the car took off—putt—putt—putt—and drove away on down the road, heading off to Delaware.

And I stood in the Go-Mart parking lot and watched them drive away. I thought, "You did the right thing Scott. You did the right thing."

But then I thought, "I guess I did the right thing?"

That's what I was telling myself at the kitchen table a couple of hours later when I went back home. "He looked so sad."

My mother piddled around in the kitchen and said, "Oh Scott. It could have been Jesus."

I told her maybe so.

Then I told her about all that had happened. I told her that he asked for fifty dollars, but I gave him seventy-five because I didn't think fifty dollars was very much by the time he got to Delaware.

Then I told her, "I guess I did the right thing."

She just patted me on the back and said, "Oh you're a good person Scott. You really are. We don't realize how responsible we are for each other. Only a good person wonders if they did the right thing."

I agreed with her.

So over the next couple of days, I told everybody I knew about what I did and they all said the same thing—that I was a good person. I told them about how Randy lost his brother. I told them about how he asked for fifty, and how I gave him seventy-five. I told them about how I doubted him, and how we were all responsible for each other.

Then about a couple of weeks later I was out at a party in Rupert with a couple of friends of mine. There was my friend Wayne, and Wayne's woman, and my friend Kevin, and this teenage girl he was dating who wasn't even out of high school yet, and who Kevin later got pregnant. He was already the father of three other children with three other girls. My friend B.J. was there too. We were all sitting on Wayne's porch, drinking beer, and telling stories back and forth to one another. Then somebody started telling a story about Randy Doogan and how crazy he was. They told how they were going down the road with their mom one day and they saw Randy fucking this girl on a picnic table, right beside the road, and how his mother pretended like she didn't see it, even though she did. He told us that it was weird to drive down the road and see a guy fucking a girl on a picnic table. And then everybody laughed. Then B.J. told us how a couple months ago he saw Randy getting his ass kicked up the sidewalk by this guy, and Randy's head was all cut up. Then everybody laughed more.

So I waited for the moment to die down so I could tell my own story. I wanted to tell them about how he lost his brother, and how I gave him some money. And finally the laughter died down and I thought, "Here's my chance."

I said, "Well it's horrible what happened to his brother."

Everybody just looked real confused and then B.J. said, "What do you mean? What are you talking about?"

I drank my beer and said, "Didn't you hear? He got killed in a car accident a couple of weeks ago. Isn't that horrible?"

But B.J. just laughed and said, "No he didn't. He didn't get killed in a car accident. Randy was going around telling everybody that and asking for money. Some dumbass even gave him some, and Randy took it and got all hopped up on dope, and ended up robbing the Handy Place. He's over in Southern Regional Jail now. He ended up knocking over some old lady on the way out and hurting her."

And then everybody laughed and started telling other stories about Randy, but I didn't. I just sat around and drank the rest of my beer, and that evening after we were all drunk, I wandered around the front yard, beside the old dozer, and emptied my pockets of a couple of dimes, and a few wadded up dollars, pieces of torn receipts, and some stupid pennies. I told myself to forget about all the old stories, and that I wasn't an asshole. As I did it, I threw some more money on the ground, and crushed it down into the rocky mud with my dirty boots. I reminded myself that I was a good person, and I was never going to do another nice thing for as long as I lived.

ODB, THE MUD PUPPY, AND ME

You ever hit a deer before? I used to ride to school in the mornings with these guys who worked at the saw mill in Princeton. There was my neighbor who everybody called ODB, and there was this other guy who everybody called the Mud Puppy and who got his name from throwing a water-dog across the river. They used to drive me to school every Monday morning at about four o'clock on their way to the saw mill.

One day we were driving through the dark woods on this old back road, listening to the Mud Puppy tell about how this guy got killed the other morning trying to miss a deer and what ODB should do if he saw one.

"Yeah most people get scared as shit and just slam on their brakes and end up getting killed," the Mud Puppy said. "What you should do is just hit the gas when you see one and use your bumper like a battering ram"

And then the Mud Puppy told us that the problem was the damn deer were all doing it on purpose. He told us that the deer are all just waiting out in the woods trying to find a car to run in front of so they can watch it crash. He told us that people are just too kind-hearted to see it. He told us deer are crazy fuckers.

Then he asked me what I thought about it, but I just smiled from the backseat and told him I didn't know.

Then ODB told him that he didn't know either.

He liked to sit outside in the mornings and watch the deer eating in the field below his house.

He said, "I figure that people just don't want to hurt something that's all pretty and wild. I know I kind of like to drink my coffee in the mornings and just watch them. It makes me feel calm."

The Mud Puppy shook his head all disgusted and told us that

deer were just rats with big eyes.

ODB chuckled and drank his coffee and drove and drove and after a while it got quiet because it was still only four o'clock in the morning and people were still sleepy. ODB pushed his Roy D. Mercer tape into the tape player and chuckled along. The tape played like it did every Monday morning and the Mud Puppy took off his sweatshirt and made a pillow out of it and propped his head up against the window. I sat in the back of the car and looked out at the dark woods and thought about all the deer waiting for us in the trees, waiting to try and take our lives.

Was that one?

Is that one?

Then I saw our headlights and a couple of deer crossing in front of us. ODB saw them too and stomped on the brakes.

EEEEEKKKK.

And then—BAM.

But it was too late. We slammed into a deer that bounced against the hood, and slid up against the window, and then shot up and over the car until it landed in the road behind us.

"Holy shit," ODB said, stopping the car in the middle of the back road.

"Holy shit," I said, grabbing a hold of the side of the car.

"Did you fuck up your car?" the Mud Puppy asked, jumping up out of his seat and staring at the hood.

Then ODB said that he knew it was bound to happen, especially with us talking about it so much. Then the car was completely stopped and he was looking back to see if he could see the deer.

I turned around too and looked at the dead deer behind us. It looked like it was dead.

"Is it dead?" I asked, looking for the deer to move. There was a big dent on the hood.

ODB shook his head like he didn't know, and the Mud Puppy looked at the hood.

Then he laughed and told us that we should have sped up. We should have done what he said.

So I asked again, "Is it dead?"

Then the deer moved its head up and down. It looked like a doe who was a couple of years old.

ODB said, "No it's not dead."

Then he turned around and his voice sounded sad. "I think I broke its back."

He broke its back and now the deer kicked its head up and down and all around. Then ODB shook his head and whispered again, "Poor thing."

And with that the Mud Puppy just popped his head around and said, "You got any rope around here, so we can put it up across the hood? We can check it after work."

But ODB just shook his head and told us that we couldn't do that. He told us we had to put it out of its misery, and we weren't putting any deer across his hood.

Then he put the car into reverse.

He hit the gas, and backed all the way up over the deer—Kabump.

The Mud Puppy jumped back like "What the hell?" as the car bounced over the deer.

"Did that do it?" ODB asked all nervous, looking back.

I looked to see if the deer was moving and at first the deer didn't move and looked like it was dead. But then the deer moved again and it was still alive. It was trying to crawl away.

So ODB put the car into drive and ran back over it again, except this time it didn't work either.

"What are you doing?" The Mud Puppy screamed, holding on to the dash.

And then the deer kicked its head some more and groaned, "Grrr" and it still wasn't dead. I told ODB, "It's still moving."

ODB looked behind the car with a look on his face like nothing should suffer more than it has to.

"What are you gonna do?" I asked.

ODB acted like he was scared and looked around the car for something to put the deer out of its misery.

He looked in the glove box for a fishing knife he kept, but it wasn't there.

He looked in the backseat for a box cutter, but there was too much trash.

He looked underneath the seat for something, but there wasn't anything there either.

There wasn't anything except his shiny thermos he drank his coffee out of in the morning.

He took his thermos and got out of the car and walked all the way back to the deer. Then the Mud Puppy looked like "What the hell is he doing?"

He said, "He's crazy—we should just leave it. It'll die sooner or later."

But I didn't care anymore. I was watching ODB stand in front of the deer holding his thermos. Then I jumped in my seat because the deer started thrashing all wild. It stood up on its front hooves, like it was trying to get away and went AHHHHH. It stood for a second and then fell back down. But ODB didn't move, and reached out with his hand and touched the side of the deer. Then he patted its side like he was trying to comfort it.

The deer rested back down like it was finally calm. ODB took his thermos, and raised it high above his head and hit the deer with it.

The Mud Puppy shook his head again like "What the hell?" watching ODB hit the deer. Then ODB hit it again.

And then again.

And then again.

But the deer wouldn't die.

It tried getting away with its broken back and ended up dragging itself into a ditch beside the road.

ODB hit it again.

"Crazy bastard," Mud Puppy said, shaking his head. "What the hell does he think he's doing?"

I decided I'd heard enough from the Mud Puppy even if he was twenty years older than me.

I told him that ODB didn't want to just leave it there with a broken back.

I told him he was trying to put it out of its misery and keep it from suffering, and he was just trying to do the right thing.

The Mud Puppy chuckled and gave me a look like, "Oh really."

But it didn't matter anymore because the deer had stopped moving. It was finally still as I watched another deer watching from the woods.

And we were all watching ODB now—the deer, and the dead deer, the Mud Puppy, and the trees, and me. We were all watching him as he touched the side of the dead deer one more time and the deer looked thankful. ODB walked back to the car, cradling the thermos to his stomach, and got in. He sat for a second and held his thermos in his arms like a child. Then the Mud Puppy looked at him all disgusted. ODB looked around the car and put his metal thermos up on the dashboard where it shined in the morning sun still rising. It shined all broken and dented at the bottom, covered in hair and blood. And ODB put the car into drive and we took off through the woods, wondering if this is what you called kindness or not.

THE RAINELLE STORY

I grew up in western Greenbrier County, West Virginia in a town called Rainelle. If I had to tell you about Rainelle, I would tell you about the weirdness. I'd tell you about One Armed Johnny and how he lost his arm. They didn't call him One Armed Johnny back then.

They just called him Johnny.

He worked at the Meadow River Lumber Co. which was the largest hardwood saw mill in the world.

He used to pull green chain, which is where they put all the new timber through the blades for the first time.

One day Johnny was pulling green chain, walking the green timber down the conveyor and running it through the buzz saw buzzing bzzzz.

And then he did it again.

He walked the timber down the conveyor and ran it through the buzz saw buzzing buzz.

And then he did it again.

He walked the timber down the conveyor....

There were these other guys working with him too.

There was Robert the cussingest man at the mill who never said a complete sentence in his whole life that didn't contain the word "shit" or "fuck."

There was the Pregnant Man and this guy named Holiday who used to go to the shitter so much they put this sign up above the toilet that said, "The Holiday Inn."

So Johnny pulled the timber through the big bad blades when cussing Robert started giving Johnny a hard time and torturing him like he always did.

He walked right up behind Johnny and reared back and socked him harder than shit in his right arm.

SMACK.

Then Robert laughed and everybody else laughed too and pointed at Johnny. But Johnny put his head down and didn't say a thing, even though his arms were always covered in black and blue bruises.

He grabbed hold of another piece of green timber and ran it through the saw.

Then he did it again.

But then a couple of minutes later Robert came up behind him again and reared back with his fist and socked him even harder this time.

SMACK.

And then everybody laughed again and Robert reached into Johnny's shirt pocket and pulled out a cigarette and put it in his own shirt pocket beside the lighter he stole off Johnny a couple of months earlier.

But Johnny didn't say anything.

He just turned towards them all and stared at Robert who laughed along with all the other guys as they all went back to pulling green chain.

But Johnny didn't. He grinned a strange grin and moved closer to the conveyor belt. He moved closer and then closer and then closer.

And that's when it happened.

The belt caught the shirt sleeve and pulled his arm into the saw. Then it ripped his right arm right off below the shoulder—just like that.

When Johnny looked down at his right arm, he expected to see his arm hanging there. But it wasn't like it was his right arm anymore. It was just this empty space and the end of a jagged bone where his right arm used to be.

So he stood for a second and watched his right arm gushing blood.

He looked back at Robert and watched him shriek. Then all shit broke lose.

Holiday ran over and shut the saw down.

Then the Pregnant Man ran over to the main office to call for help with his big beer belly bouncing all the way.

Robert shook scared wondering what to do.

But Johnny didn't.

He looked down at his missing right arm again and then at Robert.

And then Robert whispered, "Oh darn. O darn."

Of course, Johnny wasn't listening to any of this now.

He was just watching Robert's mouth moving scared. And it kept moving too, as Johnny walked over to the side of the building and sat down on an old folding chair. It was the chair Robert always sat at during their lunch breaks whispering words to Johnny like "queer."

Everyone else ran around screaming and shouting and shouting and screaming.

Then Robert followed the blood trail over to Johnny and picked up an old towel. And then he knelt in front of Johnny and tried to put the towel around the bloody stump, but there was so much blood and Robert's hands were shaking bad.

So Robert gagged gah and then he started crying.

Finally he was able to wrap the towel around the wound and try to get the blood to stop squirting.

"Oh gosh," Robert repeated as Johnny sat waiting for the ambulance to come.

And then Johnny looked at Robert and asked him like it was nothing, "Can I have a cigarette?"

Robert gave him one. He reached into his shirt pocket with his left hand and pulled out the stolen cigarette. He packed the end—pack, pack—and pushed it into Johnny's mouth. Then Robert took out his lighter and tried lighting it for him.

Light.

Nothing.

Light.

Nothing.

But then finally the lighter lit and the cigarette smoked. Robert put it back in his pocket with his shaky hands. Johnny leaned back smoking on his cigarette and smiling at his stolen lighter.

And then he was peaceful.

He sat and watched all the other guys standing around screaming and crying and cussing like they were scared. And then Johnny looked up at the pine trees, away from the sawmill and listened to the fire truck sirens blaring from the distance. He puffed on his cigarette some more and blew the smoke in a real slooooooooowwwwww stream.

He smoked his cigarette and held it in his left hand and said, "It's a beautiful evening. You know I've never seen such a beautiful evening before."

And so he sat and smoked his cigarette some more and watched the sun go down.

And that's what I'd tell you if I had to tell you about Rainelle.

I'd tell you all about pulling green chain, and the Meadow River Lumber Co. and Johnny who was Johnny once and then was Johnny no more.

I'd tell you about how he walks the streets now, searching for nickels in empty phone booths.

I'd tell you about the cigarette smoke and Robert sitting scared and sobbing, trying to keep his hands from shaking.

And then I'd tell you about those last few minutes when Johnny was just sitting in the chair waiting so peaceful.

He wasn't crying or complaining or screaming or puking or praying to God, but for the first time in his life he felt something.

He felt happy.

And so he sat and smoked his cigarette, waiting for the ambulance to come.

THE HOMELESS GUY

It wasn't my fault he threw a sandwich at my car. That afternoon I was just trying to get to work as fast as I could because I was late. I was driving down a chughole road and passing in between all of the cars, when the stop light turned red and I stopped. Shit.

So I whispered, "Come on. Come on."

That's when I saw him.

It was this homeless guy I knew. He had to have been about sixty years old, standing in front of the old homeless shelter, wearing this ratty old gray coat he always wore. He had a big bushy white beard that had a yellow tint to it. And he was holding a loaf of bread in one hand and this bologna sandwich in the other.

I guess they gave it to him in the homeless shelter.

I pulled up to the stoplight, right in front of the homeless shelter and he started shouting something at me in his homeless person talk. He pointed his sandwich at me and kept shouting.

I'd had a run in with him at the public library just a couple of days before when I didn't give him any change.

Now he started throwing his shoulders forward like he was going to kick my car's ass. I sat and thought, I've had enough of this. I wasn't going to let him kick my car's ass.

And with that I just raised my right hand and flipped him off with a real old-fashioned, middle finger, Fuck You. He didn't react like most people did when I used the middle finger.

He wasn't like the snotty-nosed kid in the drive thru at the bank who kept making faces at me and then made faces no more.

He wasn't like the WJLS radio Big Dawg mascot who just stopped waving at traffic and dropped his head in defeat.

This was a guy who got all pissed off even more and raised the bologna sandwich he was holding in his right hand and threw it at my car as hard as he could.

Shoooooo—it flew through the air almost in slow motion. I watched it fly and I thought, "That bastard is throwing a bologna sandwich at my car."

It twisted and it turned. It twisted and it turned, sailing through the air until it started sailing back down and then finally went— SPLAT—against the hood of my car. Then it sat on the hood like a wet rag. I looked at the homeless guy and then the homeless guy looked at me.

I threw open the car door even though the light had changed green and I screamed, "I'll get you, you son of a bitch. I'll get you for throwing a bologna sandwich at my car." I was crazy.

But the homeless guy didn't even hear me because he took off running like a fucking track star or something. A couple of the other homeless guys who were just hanging out laughed at me too.

It wasn't a couple of weeks later after my girlfriend's mom came to visit us for the weekend that I saw him again. For some reason or another we decided to walk around town and show Kim's mom where we lived and impress her and let her know it was all right that her nineteen-year-old daughter was living with me. We started on our walk down the street and I saw him rumbling and bumbling up the sidewalk all drunk as hell.

I shook my head and thought, "What ever you do Scott, don't lose your temper. Don't even think about him throwing that bologna sandwich at your car. Kim's mom is here and you're trying to impress her."

I was going to let him pass by and deal with it on another day, when all of the sudden he reached out with his gnawed up hand (like he didn't even recognize me) and started talking his drunk talk and demanding money. He hit me in the chest with his hand.

I could tell he was scaring Kim's mom, so I pushed him out of the way and said, "Get out of here buddy."

He fell back a step and shouted, "Well fuck you, motherfucker."

So I got up in his face and was like "What?"

He shouted again, "Well fuck you, motherfucker."

Kim said, "Let's just keep walking, Scott. Just forget about it. It's not that big of a deal."

And then Kim's mom pretended like it wasn't even happening

and started saying, "Oh this is such a cute little town. It's just so cute."

But I couldn't let it go.

I pushed him again and then he grabbed a hold of my shirt and then I shoved him and said, "You're the bastard who threw the sandwich at my car for no reason. Don't nobody throw a bologna sandwich at my car and use that kind of language in front of women. You piece of shit."

So the homeless guy and I started wrestling back and forth, holding onto each other's arms and I was shouting, "You're not going to use that kind of language."

And he held onto my arm and kept repeating, "Fuck you, motherfucker."

And now Kim was pleading, desperate. "Please Scott, let's go. Please."

But it was too late because now we were on the ground wrestling around. I was shouting about the bologna sandwich, and he was shouting his drunk shouts and Kim was shouting. "No Scott. No. My mother's here. You're embarrassing me."

But I wouldn't listen to her. I punched him awkwardly in the chest. And then he hit me on top of the head. Then we were rolling around and around in each other's arms and he was pulling on my shirt and I was gagging from the smell of his shit-stained trousers. This went on for about a minute, but I couldn't get a good punch in. Then he got up somehow and took off running fast as hell.

I got up too and giggled at what a coward he was and dusted off my pants and straightened up my shirt and shouted at him, "Yeah you bastard. When I see you again I'm going to kick your ass."

And then I turned around and Kim and her mom were just standing there shocked.

Kim was holding her face and crying and her mother was looking at me like, "What's wrong with you? Really, what's wrong with you?"

Then later that night, after Kim's mom went to bed, I kept trying to explain myself. It made me feel good about myself. It made me feel good to beat that dude's ass.

Kim just snapped, "Oh shit Scott. It's not like it was even a fight really. It was more like a wrestling match. The guy obviously has something wrong with him and you didn't care. He just took off running because he was afraid the cops were coming."

Then she was quiet and whispered, "And besides that, my mother thinks you have anger issues now."

But I didn't care.

I didn't have anger issues.

I just wanted to go find him and make him pay for throwing the sandwich at my car. Over the next couple of months I started looking for him everywhere. I started going down to the public library and hanging out all day, but I never once saw him there either. So then, every day when I drove home, I came up the road, hoping I'd see him pushing his buggy or drinking his 24 ounce can wrapped in a brown paper bag, but he wasn't there either. I started going down to the Riverfront Park in the evenings and waited in my car, hoping he might show up.

But he wasn't there either.

It was like he was just gone.

And by this time there were other things gone too. My girlfriend Kim had moved out and was dating a new boyfriend.

I was going to be homeless soon because the lease was up on the apartment and things were all going to hell.

One day right before I left town, I walked down to the Riverfront Park and sat down on an old bench and drank a 40 ounce of beer, thinking I might see him still. I hadn't shaved in about a week. I'd been wearing the same jeans for about three weeks until they were all greasy. I figured I'd look for him one more time and hope he'd show up. So I pulled out an old hamburger I'd bought after I scraped together about two dollars worth of nickels and dimes. I unwrapped the hamburger and took a bite out of it and washed it down with a gulp of beer. I sat and watched the river roll all dirty and full of dead things, and then I saw this group of people walking up the river. At first I thought it was the cops so I made sure I covered up my beer so I wouldn't get busted for an open container.

But then they walked closer and closer and they were laughing and having a good time. It was girls and guys, laughing and telling jokes and giggling at how funny the world was. And as they passed by my bench that's when I saw him. It was the homeless guy or at least it kind of looked like the homeless guy, except he looked all different now. His hair was cut short and combed over, and his beard was shaved off, but the eyes were the same somehow.

I wanted to shout and scream at him and throw my beer bottle at him and tell him I remembered what he did. I remember how he threw the sandwich at me and made me look like a fool in front of my woman, but I didn't.

I didn't because I couldn't even tell if it was the same guy even. This guy looked twenty years younger.

He was dressed up in a shirt and tie, and he wasn't alone.

Then they saw me and looked at me and I guess I looked kind of funny to them. I was trying to hide the beer bottle from them and balance my Wendy's hamburger at the same time. A couple of them pointed their fingers at me and started laughing.

But the homeless guy didn't. He just grinned at me and smiled and I saw that his teeth weren't all rotten like I remembered. They even looked real. But the others were laughing and I felt like I was going to lose it.

I tried shouting something at them to make them stop laughing at me.

I wanted to shout something like, "I'm a human being. I haven't shaved in a week because my girlfriend broke up with me and I don't know what I'm going to do with my life now."

But when I tried to scream at them it didn't work. It all just came out in gurgles and grunts like homeless person talk. So with this they stopped laughing and they looked the other way like there was something wrong with me.

I just grunted and groaned and they walked on by because I had nothing now.

THE CHAINSAW GUY

You can see all kinds of weird shit in Rainelle. One time I was driving past the welfare apartments in town when I looked up and saw something that changed my world.

I was with my mother and we were going over the railroad tracks when I looked up and saw this guy in a red sweat suit riding a 12 speed bicycle as fast as he could down the hill.

What was even stranger was that the 12 speed bike didn't even have a chain on it. And what was even stranger than that was that he was carrying a chainsaw in his right hand. Not only was he riding a bike and carrying a chainsaw at the same time, but get this—the chainsaw was running.

We sat at the railroad tracks and I pointed to the man on the hill and asked my mother, "What in the hell is that guy doing anyway?"

My mother looked up at the guy and then she said, "I don't know."

We rolled up over the train tracks and on down the road. I twisted my head around and kept watching the guy riding his bike and carrying a chainsaw.

I asked again, "Why is that guy carrying a chainsaw?"

My mother just shook her head and said, "I don't know. I really don't."

And by this time we were driving on down the road, and I couldn't see him anymore. I knew there was something about him that meant something, and if I ever found out what it was—then maybe I'd finally know the meaning of my life.

THE FIRESTARTER

I went through this weird period about ten years ago where every time I went outside, I saw somebody get hit by a car. The first time it ever happened I was just sitting around my apartment and listening to the drunks shouting from the bar next door. It was Labor Day weekend and I was sitting on the couch watching television. I was just about ready to go to bed when all the sudden—BAM. I heard this big thud outside. I looked out the window and opened the door, but I didn't see anything. There were cars in the bar parking lot and this flashing light.

My girlfriend Kim woke up and walked into the room and said, "What the hell was that?"

"I don't know," I said.

She pushed me out the door and said all disgusted, "Well go outside and see."

So I did.

I went outside to see, and as soon as I did, I realized it was a mistake.

There was this white van in the middle of the road with its blinkers on and there was a guy sitting on his knees in the grass. He was dressed in painter pants and he was crying. So I walked slow out into the street and saw this dead looking girl sprawled in the middle of the street.

Her mouth was open and her eyes were too.

She didn't even look like she was breathing and there was this dead look on her face.

The guy who hit her was sitting there, looking up at me and crying like, "What are you going to do?"

I looked down at the girl and guess what? She still looked dead to me. Her mouth was still open and there was blood coming out of the corner of her mouth.

Since I'd never taken a CPR class before, I just kept looking and thought, "What the hell am I going to do?"

I started backing up, real slow so I wouldn't have to help her.

Back. Back. Back.

Then I turned around and started walking away even faster like I didn't even know who she was.

Then her boyfriend and another guy ran back out. They were with her when she was hit and went to call for help. They were these J-Crew catalog looking guys. They stared at me and so I wasn't able to get away. They bent down on their knees and started giving her CPR.

One one thousand…two one thousand…three one thousand.

Then they just looked up at me and gave me a look like "Were you trying to sneak away from helping a person?"

I walked back and acted like I was directing traffic around the girl.

I took my arm and waved the traffic on Route 60—to the left and to the left.

Then the ambulance came and I slowly backed away to the sidewalk and watched them take over the CPR. They put her on a stretcher and put her into the back of the ambulance and drove away.

Was I wrong?

Of course, a couple of weeks went by and I didn't hear anything about whether she died or not. Then one day I was walking down the street with Kim when I asked, "I wonder what happened to that girl who got hit by the car? I wonder if she's all right? You know I haven't heard anything about what happened and I kind of wonder if she died or not."

We walked on down the street and Kim was holding a newspaper and then she opened it up.

I heard her shout, "Oh shit. Here it is. She's alive. She's alive." She showed it to me. There was a picture of the girl and a headline that said, WOMAN HIT BY VAN RECOVERS.

As I checked it out, there were a couple Gideons standing around and they were trying to pass out Bibles to people who were walking down the street.

Want a Bible?

Nope.

Want a Bible?

Nope.

Want a Bible?

Nope.

Then Kim read the newspaper article to me about the girl who got hit.

She read the who, what, when, where, and why opening of the story: "Last Sunday night a twenty-three-year old woman, trying to cross the street was hit by a car on Route 60."

Then she read about how the girl had been in a coma in intensive care for the past week and had almost died, and how her family had kept a prayer vigil beside her bed.

And then one day.

TA DA.

She woke up.

Then the article explained how that the poor guy who hit her was drunk.

"Ah shit," I said and chuckled. "Poor bastard got busted and he wasn't even the one who was jaywalking."

Then there was this quote where the girl said, "I just want to thank everybody for their prayers and cards. There wasn't anything I could have done. It wasn't my fault."

I laughed out loud because it was absolutely, positively her fault.

That's when I heard the brakes shriek eeek.

I looked into the street and then—BAM. I saw another girl get hit by a car.

She was knocked to the ground and then she popped back up and took off like she was embarrassed or something.

Now let me tell you, I'm sure you may have been embarrassed before, but you haven't truly been embarrassed until you get hit by a car in front of a bunch of people.

What was funny though was the guy in the car didn't even get out of the car, but tried helping her up by putting his arm out the window. You need help?

But she was already gone and didn't want help.

What's even funnier is that the Gideons didn't even go over and help her out, but they just kept passing out Bibles like nothing had ever happened.

Want a Bible?

Nope.

Want a Bible?

Nope.

Want a Bible?

Nope.

Want a Bible?

So I kept walking up the street and I started thinking, "This is the second time this month I've been around when somebody was hit by a car. What if I'm the one who caused it?"

I even started telling my friends halfway joking, "Yeah I might be like Drew Barrymore in that movie *Firestarter*. You know the one where all she has to do is think about it and she starts a fire? Maybe that's me. All I have to do is be around and it happens. If there's one thing that connect these people getting hit by cars—it's me."

And then everyone just laughed at me thinking I was joking and then they told me nobody can change things like that.

They laughed again and told me that the world was just chance and didn't work that way.

Everybody laughed at me but I didn't.

I didn't laugh at all because I knew what I could do.

I didn't laugh at all because just a month later, I was walking down the street.

And I saw IT.

I saw this red car zipping down the street with these old people inside.

I saw this tall, lanky guy walking across the street as the stoplight turned red. He was carrying some books in his arms and he was trying to get where he was going.

I saw the red car keep going and not even notice that the light was turning.

It went GREEN and then it went YELLOW and then it went RED. And instead of screaming STOP-STOP, I didn't do anything.

I just stood and watched it all, knowing what I could do.

I just stood and saw how everything would happen. And then I said it.

I said BAM.

And BAM it was. The car plowed though the intersection and didn't even hit the brakes. I saw it all.

I saw the red car.

And the guy getting hit by the car…

The windshield shattering from a big leg busting against it…

The body flying through the air like an old sock…

And then…

Falling…

Falling…

Back down onto the hood of the red car.

And then there were people running around.

They were screaming.

The headline in the newspaper a couple of days later: MAN NEAR DEATH CROSSING THE STREET.

I didn't even stop because I was the one who caused it. I didn't even stop and just kept walking beneath the sound of the people screaming for help.

I went right back to my apartment and shut the door. I locked the lock and closed the blinds and told myself I would never go outside again. I turned on the television and turned the volume up real loud so I wouldn't have to listen to the sounds of the girl having sex upstairs. I just sat and listened to the sound of the television drowning out everything and for a second it didn't even seem like daytime anymore, but night. And then I told myself that I'd never even tell anyone about it because I was the one who caused it. I tried shaking away the images of my friends and cars and telling them about the fires I started.

I told myself I'd tell no one, because if I did then I was probably putting their lives in danger.

And now after reading this who knows what car will be coming for you tomorrow.

THE PRETTIEST GIRL IN TEXAS

I was staying at my grandma's house in Texas that summer when something shook me awake. At first I didn't even know what was going on, so I just closed my eyes and tried going back to sleep.

But then I felt something shake me again and say, "Hey boy. Get up. I want to show you something."

It was my uncle.

My uncle was only ten years older than me, so he wasn't even like an uncle really. A couple of days earlier, he stopped by and told me we should hang out and spend some time together.

So that's why I got up out of bed now and tried looking for my shirt and pants in the darkness of my grandma's house.

Is this them?

Nope.

Is this them?

I was having trouble trying to find my things. My uncle just clicked on the light switch for me, and my wake-up eyes burned with black spots—pop pop pop.

But then I whispered, "What's going on?"

I wondered if maybe he wanted to go scuba diving in the bottom of the backyard pool or maybe just watch some TV. But he didn't say anything. I put my pants on and found my boots and asked again, "Where are we going?"

My uncle just flipped off the light switch and said, "We're going to go see THE PRETTIEST GIRL IN TEXAS."

"What?" I whispered all excited and laughed.

And then he told me how he'd seen this stripper out at a bar just a couple nights before and this is what she was calling herself. He told me how the Cowboys were in town for their training camp and they heard about her too. They brought about half the team out to see her

34

and he'd never seen anything like it. He'd never seen such a bunch of guys with their mouths so open. She was dressed in a cheerleader outfit and everyone was stunned. STUNNED. STUNNED.

So I finished putting on my clothes and followed him out to his truck and got in beside him, imagining what she looked like.

I imagined her in a blue Dallas Cowboys cheerleader outfit with silver tassels.

I imagined the white and blue pom poms bouncing back and forth.

I imagined the white boots and the white jacket and the high leg kicks.

Then I imagined what she looked like without these things.

I finally stopped imagining it all, as we took off down the road, and I thought about what my mom always said about this part of Texas, "Oh Godforsaken land. I don't know why anybody would want to live out here."

I whispered this to myself as we drove for a half hour through the dust, past the oil wells, and then down a rutty old back road, which kicked up even more dust and made the truck go bounce, bounce, bounce, until we finally pulled up to this double wide trailer, covered in Christmas lights and with a shack built on the side of it.

There was a sign out front that said:
TONIGHT. THE PRETTIEST GIRL IN TEXAS. $3 DOLLAR DRAFTS.

"Well here we are," he said, stopping the truck, and grinning a shit-eating grin. "I told you."

I got out of the truck and walked towards the front door and went inside. There was probably about eight or nine folks hanging around inside.

There was an old woman serving drinks, and a couple of rednecks in cowboy hats. There was a chubby salesman talking up a storm and somebody's little daughter sitting up on top of a broken pinball machine. The little girl was eating one of those orange push up thingies. There was a Mexican girl up front dancing on the stage to a slow country song.

"Is this a strip club?" I asked, confused because I'd never really seen one before, let alone been in one.

My uncle just took a long drag off his cigarette and said, "Kinda."

So we sat down at a table and my uncle held up two fingers for them to bring him some beer and waited for the prettiest girl in Texas to come on.

But right then there was just the Mexican girl dancing back and forth on the tiny stage.

Then there was another girl over on the other side of the stage dancing too, except she looked fucked up. Her eyes were all glazed over and there was this burn all the way down her shoulder like somebody had spilled a hot pot of coffee on her. I sat and watched the girls as they kept dancing on the crappy, makeshift stage, back and forth, and up and down.

I asked my uncle, "What's wrong with their eyes?"

My uncle couldn't hear me because of the music.

So I asked again, "What's wrong with their eyes?"

He just squinted and looked up at her. "Oh they're high. Haven't you ever seen somebody high before?"

I didn't say anything.

I sat and watched them dance some more and start taking off their tops, but I couldn't hardly look at them I was so uncomfortable. I'd only seen a naked woman a couple of times before anyway. The first time was at my buddy's house, when his mom came out of the shower one day not knowing we were inside. Then there was another time, one summer, when I played spotlight with this chubby girl in the woods. So now, I tried playing it cool and imagined what the prettiest girl in Texas was going to look like. I imagined the silver tassels, and the white boots, and the white and blue pom poms.

Then the song ended and the girls left the stage.

It was quiet and my uncle smiled. He said, "You ready?"

I was ready and the people in the bar were too. So we waited.

We waited and then the place went black. Another country song started playing. It was quiet and then the spotlight shined on the stage and showed the outline of a woman's face.

It was her.

THE PRETTIEST GIRL IN TEXAS.

She didn't look like the other girls though. She was older than the rest of them and real skinny, so skinny that her long neck looked even longer. She had a stripper outfit like a Dallas Cowboys cheerleader all right, but she didn't have any pom poms at all. And her white boots just looked all dirty, scuffed up, and old. When the spotlight pulled back she was standing with her right shoulder to us, snapping her fingers and swaying back and forth in her cheerleading costume. And that's when I saw it.

She didn't have an arm, except for a stub that ended just above the elbow. She was wearing a sock on the stub with a little pasty at the end. I understood.

This was the whole act. She didn't take off any of her clothes, but she just kept pulling on the sock real sexy like. At first I didn't know what to think. The prettiest girl in Texas just kept shaking her stub up on the stage so that the tassels flipped, and flopped, and twirled around and around like a propeller. My uncle lit another cigarette and watched her like there was nothing unusual about this. Then he leaned over and told me about what had happened to her.

She was sixteen years old and riding a motorcycle.

A truck was coming.

It was raining.

There was screeching.

Brakes.

A crash.

The bike went sliding down the road in a trail of sparks.

Flying.

And they found her about half an hour later in a mesquite bush.

After he told me this, he leaned back in the chair and watched her some more. I watched her too. I watched her keep reaching over and pulling at the end of the sock. By this time it was like the music wasn't playing anymore. There was just the woman, pulling on the sock. Then she stopped. She just pulled on the sock some more, but real slow and drawn out. Then she did it one more time, and it came off, and she was just standing in front of us all, holding the sock in her hand and letting her bare nub hang free.

My uncle leaned over and whispered, "This is what I wanted to show you. This."

I looked over at him thinking he was going to laugh somehow and this was all a joke. But it wasn't a joke because there was sadness in his face.

There was sadness in everybody's face—the little girl sitting on the pinball machine, the old woman who served the beer, the girl who was dancing with the fucked up eyes. They sat and watched her and they all looked so sad and missing something, all of them except for the prettiest girl in Texas. She just took her sock and twirled it above her head. And then she pointed her arm at us and wiggled it around and round in little circles like she was trying to hypnotize us and tell us that we were the ones who were naked.

And after watching her wiggle her arm for a couple of minutes I was ready to tell her she wasn't the prettiest girl in Texas anymore.

I was ready to tell her she was the most beautiful woman in the world.

THE BABY DOLL

I never should have listened to them. I was in the 4ᵗʰ grade and we were getting ready for the Christmas play. It was a play the whole class was going to put on where we dressed up like toys and sang songs beneath a Christmas tree.

All of the guys in the class were sitting around talking about what kind of toys they should dress up like.

Should I be a G.I. Joe?

Should I be a football player?

Should I be a cowboy?

I was going to dress up like a football player too, but then Ammie, this cute girl in our class, said, "Why don't you dress up like baby dolls? It'll be funny."

A couple of the guys laughed about how funny it was and then my buddy Jay said, "Yeah why don't we? Why don't we dress up like baby dolls?"

My friend Mike said, "Yeah let's do it."

Ammie's friend Nicole went, "Please, Please."

Then Carrie said, "Please, Please."

Then Jay said again, "Yeah let's do it."

And then they looked at me, but I didn't want to.

I wanted to dress up like a football player. I knew you had to be careful doing these kinds of things. I remember my 5ᵗʰ birthday party when I asked for Barbie dolls and the Barbie doll swimming pool (not because I wanted the pool but because I wanted to drink the water from the pool) and all of my uncles just shook their heads when I opened up my Barbie.

They said, "Yeah. That's not right."

So I knew that you had to be careful doing stuff like this.

Jay said, "What are you, chicken?"

I said, "No."

Mike said, "Are you chicken?"

I finally said, "Okay. I'll do it."

Jay said, "Well you better. I don't want to show up this evening and be the only one dressed up."

I still wasn't sure if I was going to do it or not, even after I told my mom about it when I got home.

She laughed and thought it was a great idea.

"Oh gracious Scott. That's such a great idea. You guys will be the cutest things there." Before I knew it we were in the bedroom and she was getting out a pair of her old pantyhose. Then she was getting out one of her maternity dresses and clipping the bottom of it. Before I knew it I was wearing this pair of pantyhose, and I was wearing my mom's ratty dress. We laughed and looked in the mirror just like when I was a little boy and she dressed me up like a girl before my dad came home.

We looked in the mirror and she put the lipstick on me and then two big red spots on my cheeks.

"Oh Scott you look so cute," she said and handed me one of my baby rattles.

She put a bow in my hair and said, "Do you feel cute?"

And guess what?

I did.

I stood in front of the long mirror in my pantyhose and my dress.

I swirled the dress around me and I touched the bow in my hair and for the first time in my life I felt cute. For the first time in my life I felt beautiful.

I was still feeling beautiful when I showed up at school that evening and walked to the music room in my doll baby shoes. My dad shook his head with another "That boy's not right." I walked into the music room and everybody started laughing. My friend Mike wasn't dressed up like a baby doll. He was dressed up like a G.I. Joe. His face was painted with camouflage face paint. When he saw me he started laughing too.

He said, "I can't believe you did it. What were you thinking?"

I looked at him and said, "I thought we were all going to dress up like baby dolls."

I thought we agreed to it. He laughed.

I thought, "Well at least I can still count on Jay."

I knew Jay would be dressed up too.

But then Jay came walking through the door and he wasn't dressed up like a baby doll either. He was dressed up like a G.I. Joe.

I looked at them and said, "I thought we were all going to dress up like baby dolls." Jay laughed at me.

Then Michael laughed at me. I was still pissed off, and shook my head at what a bunch of pussies they all were. Pussies. They wouldn't say anything. They kept laughing and playing with the bow in my hair and touching my dress and smearing my lip stick like jerks. I tried knocking their hands away but they wouldn't stop laughing and touching my dress. Besides that, it was time for us to go to the gym and get ready for the Christmas play.

We walked over to the gym and sat down on the risers with the big purple curtain closed in front of us. I sat down beside Ammie who was dressed up like a princess and listened to all of the parents talking outside.

Ammie leaned over and said, "Don't let those guys bother you. You look beautiful in your dress. You really do."

I shook my head, "Yeah" because I thought so too.

We all sat on the riser along with all the other toys waiting for the curtains to open. And then they did.

And then it was quiet for a second.

But then....

There was a giggle.

There were two giggles and then there was a whole gym full of people laughing. They were pointing their fingers at me and I could read their lips. They were laughing, "Look at that little boy dressed up like a girl."

There were people taking pictures of me instead of taking pictures of their own kids.

Snap. Snap.

They were taking pictures of the beautiful baby doll.

Snap.

I sat in the bleacher beside Ammie and let the people take pictures of me.

"It's a boy dressed up like a girl."

I sang along to the Christmas pageant songs and tried to disappear.

I didn't feel cute in my baby doll clothes anymore, and besides that I was shivering. I was cold.

I was so cold that there were goose bumps bumping up on my legs.

I tried scooting closer to Ammie. She put her arm around me and tried warming me up, and I felt myself getting smaller. Before long it was like I wasn't even there anymore.

It was like I was gone.

So after it was all over, I ran back out to the car in the snow and tried getting in before anyone could see me. Jay was walking behind me too. I saw him watching me wiggle and jiggle in my baby doll dress, and it looked like he liked the way I walked. He picked up a snow ball and tried throwing it at me—BAM. But it missed. And then I was in the car and my parents were with me and we were driving all the way back home. At home my mother helped me take the bow out of my hair. She helped me take out my clip-on earrings.

She helped wipe some of my makeup off and said, "You remember when we used to play dress up when you were a little boy?"

And I giggled, "Yeah."

She said, "You remember when we used to dress you up like a little girl and then fix you up like a vampire?"

I said, "Yeah."

Then she helped me take off her maternity dress and I just stood without anything on except for my white pantyhose.

"You know I never got a chance to have a little girl—but you were the prettiest one there tonight. I always wanted a girl."

By this time I was sick of talking about it.

I stood in my white pantyhose and my red lipstick. And then I went and sat down in front of the TV and watched this Vietnam War show on CBS called *Tour of Duty*.

I watched the G.I. Joe guys in camouflage shooting machine guns in the jungle.

I watched a man take a knife and stab a Viet Cong.

I watched a soldier get shot and start dying as the helicopter came down to pick the soldier up.

I watched the helicopter lift up as the Viet Cong shot all around it.

Then Zeke, the platoon leader, called in an air strike and there were explosions and bombs blowing up, and hand grenades exploding, and things dying. And so I just sat in my white pantyhose and my red lipstick and I imagined myself a soldier in some far away land, searching for something beautiful to kill.

PHONE GIRL

It started with the phone call. I was sitting in my room not doing a damn thing when the phone went—ring, ring—and I picked it up, expecting it to be one of my friends.

"Hello." I said, but there wasn't any voice on the other line. There was just this heavy breathing.

I said, "Hello" again thinking it was a telemarketer, when the voice on the other line started giggling.

"Hello," I said again.

"Who the hell is this?" I said, going through all the people it could be.

Could it be Wayne? No, he was in basic training by now.

Could it be Randy? No, he was in jail for his third DUI.

Then the voice on the other line said, "What are you wearing?"

And I giggled too, not recognizing the voice at all.

She giggled and I giggled back.

She said, "Who is this?"

I tried thinking up a name I could tell her.

Eric.

John.

Bill.

George.

I said, "George," and as soon as I said it I thought, "God, George sounds like a made up name."

She realized it too and said, "George of the Jungle."

Then she breathed sexy and said, "Okay George what's your real name?"

I couldn't take it anymore. I asked her who put her up to this. I knew somebody was listening on the other line. But she didn't say anything and I believed her. I believed her and told her my name was

Scott. She grew quiet and said, "Okay Scott. It's your lucky day. Do you know what I'm doing right now?"

I sure as hell didn't and felt my breath growing heavy. I didn't care if it was a prank phone call or not, my hand was shaking so bad.

And then she said that she just wanted me to know that she was alone and then she started groaning.

She breathed heavy again and I realized she wasn't joking. She moaned again. I sat in my chair and listened to her on the phone and then I thought—what the hell! This is my lucky day. She started moaning and groaning and groaning and moaning. And I imagined her bed and her body and her blonde hair.

I thought whatever floats your boat. I enjoyed it. It was all over a couple of minutes later and she said goodbye and hung up.

After that a week or so went by and I didn't hear from her. She called again one day and she moaned some more. She called the next day and did the same thing. Then she hung up. But then the next day the phone rang and I picked it up and we just talked. I found out all kinds of stuff about her. I found out her real name was Jacqueline and she was twenty-two years old and worked as a secretary in a law office. She was paid like shit, but she just broke up with her boyfriend because he beat her.

He beat the hell out of her.

She told me she was a blonde in a bottle and 5'6".

I told her what I looked like too.

Then she whispered like usual, "I want you."

That's the way it was. She giggled and said this was the strangest relationship in the history of relationships. We both laughed and talked about all kinds of things.

We talked about how hard it was to meet somebody in this world who you can connect with, and even sometimes when you think you found someone you really haven't found the person, but just the idea of the person. Then we talked about how weird it was she just called a number up out of the blue because she was bored and had nothing to do. We talked about how maybe she didn't even exist, and maybe we were just a figment of each other's imagination. She told me even though we'd never seen each other's faces—she saw who I was. She said that most people see faces and don't know anything else. She breathed heavy and asked me who I was. I told her. I told her I was a twenty-two-year-old guy and I'd never even had a girlfriend really. I told her I was so lonely there was a fly living in my room for a couple of days and I couldn't kill it. I told her I talked to it and pretended it talked to me.

I said, "Are you lonely little fly?"

I said, "Yeah I'm lonely too."

Then we laughed and she said I should write her a love letter. She said she would write me a love letter too.

After I got off the phone, I sat down and wrote her a love letter. I told her about how much the past couple weeks had meant to me. And then I told her that I loved talking to her. I said that I knew that this wasn't just chance. She knew me better than anyone and I was thankful for it. I thought I should take a picture of myself. I went home that weekend, and I had my mother take a picture of me without my shirt on. I put the picture in an envelope along with the letter. I finished with the letter and then at the end I wrote, "I hope this doesn't freak you out, but I love you."

When I got her letter there was a baby picture and a picture of a beautiful blonde girl. There was a letter she wrote that said, "I hope this doesn't freak you out. But I'm in love with you."

One late night after talking for about an hour, and listening to the moaning and groaning, we decided to meet up. I got in my car and drove down to a grocery store parking lot which was close to her house. I waited for her in my car. I sat out in the front seat looking around for the red sports car that she said she would be driving. She wasn't showing up so I took out the letter that said "Love, Jackie" and then...

I hunger for your cock.

I sat and chuckled and I imagined all the people. Is that her? Is that her? When I looked out of my window I saw a fat woman and I thought—Is that her? I thought of my friend who had a girl like this—only to find out it was a guy. Why would someone like this want someone like me? I sat and looked at the picture, and a half hour passed and then an hour and then an hour and a half. I drove back to my room to call her, thinking there must have been a mix-up on the meeting place.

I drove all the way back to my room and passed a man in the

street. Is that her? I picked up the phone and called her telephone number. The phone rang a couple of times and I was thinking, "Shit. She's somewhere waiting on me." But then someone picked it up and a voice said, "Hello."

It wasn't Jacqueline. It was a rough-sounding woman's voice.

"Is Jacqueline there?" I asked, wondering.

"Jacqueline. You mean Jackie?" The voice sounded confused. "I guess this is her friend from school."

"What?"

"Well this is Jackie's mom and she can't go out tonight. She's got school in the morning and she can't be going out late at night. "

I held the phone to my ear and thought, "What the hell?"

Then there were voices arguing and all of a sudden Jacqueline was on the phone sounding like she'd been crying. "What the fuck is going on?" I said.

She tried playing it off.

"Oh my roommate was being silly."

"What? Roommate? She said she was your mom."

Then Jackie giggled except it wasn't a sexy giggle anymore. It was the giggle of a little girl. I just asked her if she was twenty-two and worked in a law office like she said and she just giggled. I asked her if she was eighteen, thinking she was in high school maybe. She giggled. I felt like I was going to be sick. But I still asked her.

Sixteen.

She giggled.

Fifteen.

She giggled.

Fourteen.

She giggled.

Thirteen.

She giggled.

Twelve.

She stopped giggling. She said, "Well I'm going to be twelve in two months."

I flipped out, and she told me it was her cousin in the picture she sent and that everybody said she was going to look like that when she grew up.

I started screaming, "I can't be doing this. This is illegal." I told her I needed to stop talking to her.

She got mad.

She told me, "If you stop talking to me, I'll tell my mom. I'll tell my mom everything about the dirty talk and I'll show her your letter." She read me a raunchy sentence. My heart dropped. She whispered, "I want to hear you."

"What?"

"I want to hear you or I'll tell."

I hung up. The phone rang. Ring Ring.

I just let it ring and put my hand on the phone.

And even now, years later, when I see all the faces, I think, Is that her? I see women at the grocery store, and I see people outside. Is that her? And even now whenever the phone rings, guess what?

I still want it to be her.

MY DAD AND THE COP

I never knew why he did it. I was always afraid of my dad growing up, especially when I was in the 6th grade and we were going up Sewell Mountain with this old trellis sticking out of the back of the truck. There was my dad and my mom and me. I was holding onto my mom, trying to keep from getting sick because of my dad's crazy ass driving, and that's when it started. My dad looked into his rear view mirror and started slowing down.

My mother said, "What's wrong Gary?"

Gary Mack looked into his rearview mirror and said, "Well shit. What does he want?"

So I looked back and there was a cop behind him, following behind us and flashing his cop lights.

I thought, "Oh God, don't let anything go wrong."

The lights flashed red, clear and blue—red, clear and blue—red, clear and blue.

My dad kept driving up the side of the mountain because there really wasn't a place to pull over anymore and then he said, "Well where does that bastard think I'm going to go?"

He finally stopped in the middle of a nasty turn in the road.

He said, "I wonder if it's that trellis hanging out of the back?"

My mother said, "Yeah, I bet it's the trellis all right. It's probably just sticking out too far and he wants you to put a flag on it. He doesn't have any business stopping you on this old twisty turny road though."

I looked out the back of the truck at the trellis and the cop sitting in the car writing something.

My dad repeated, "No, he doesn't have any business at all stopping me in the middle of the mountain like this."

The copper finally quit writing and opened up the door and got out of the car. He was probably only about 5'5" and 240 pounds.

My dad just watched him in the side mirror and chuckled to himself, "Well look at that old fatty. He's about three foot tall and six foot around. I'd heard they kicked him out of the state police academy because he was so big around he couldn't fit through the front door."

My mother softly touched his arm like she always did when she was trying to calm him down and said, "Now, Gary."

Gary just kept watching the cop. The cop walked up to the door and said in his best badass police voice, "Sir I need to see your license and registration, please."

My dad looked at him like "What the hell are you talking about?"

The fat copper said, "You were speeding. I caught you going 65 in a 50."

My dad said, "What do you mean speeding? I wasn't speeding."

I thought, "Dad, why are you doing this? Why are you doing this?"

He showed my dad the ticket and said, "You'll have to sign this ticket, sir."

My dad said, "I'm not signing a damn thing buddy."

The cop grew nervous and said, "Well sir, I'll have to impound your truck and take you to jail."

My dad said, "The hell you will." He threw the keys to my mom and said, "She can drive."

"Why are you doing this dad? Why are you doing this?"

The cop got even more nervous and he said, "Well sir, I'll have to arrest you and take you to jail."

My dad opened up the door and said, "Well let's go Buddy." He got out, walked to the back of the police car, past the policeman, and opened the back door of the police car. He got in. The cop stood there and looked at my mother like he didn't know what to do, like he didn't know what to do with a guy who actually wanted to go to jail.

The cop shook his head and walked back to his car. One of our neighbors drove by and honked the horn.

Honk.

Honk.

She waved out the window and it looked like everybody in the car was laughing.

"Oh God mom, now everybody is going to know," I said, trying to duck my head. So my mom slid over in the seat and tried adjusting the seat. She was so short we had to pull it up all the way. She tried telling me to settle down. She said, "Well, you know your dad." I watched the police car turn around in the middle of the road and then my mom turned around in the middle of the road too, and I said, "Why is he doing this? Why is he doing this?"

We followed the police car down into town and towards Town Hall where the city jail was. My dad sat in the back of the police car. He told us what happened later. He said they were going down the road and the cops' radio went off because somebody had been stabbed or shot or something.

The cop picked up his radio and said, "Sorry I can't respond right now. I have a prisoner in the car."

My dad laughed and said, "Prisoner in the car."

Then he saw the town recorder coming out of the post office and said, "Well hell, there's Rip. We can take care of this right now."

The fat cop just kept driving though. My dad started mouthing, "I guess you're the type of guy they only give one bullet just in case you try shooting somebody."

They pulled in front of the town jail.

My dad said, "Dumbass."

My mom and I pulled in front of the town jail too. I sat in the truck and waited with my mom and said, "What's wrong with him? Why didn't he just sign the ticket?"

I kept going, "Why is he doing this? Why is he doing this? We were going over to grandma's to eat and now he's in jail."

My mom said, "Well he didn't have any business stopping your father on that twisty turny road. I don't see how he could have been going 65 MPH." Of course he wasn't. It was end of the month quotas.

My mom said, "I guess I should go inside and see him."

So she did. She went in to check on him, but he wouldn't come out. I went in too. My mom and I stood at the door of the jailhouse listening to the cop and the town recorder trying to talk him into just paying the speeding ticket. By this time, the cop didn't even want to fill out the paper work. He was telling dad he was going to forget the arrest, as long as he paid the ticket. Rip, the town recorder, even told my dad, "Now Mack you can't stay here. You got a family out there depending on you. Now I know we pissed you off, but you've got to go home. You can't stay in here. Your wife and your child are waiting on you."

But my dad wouldn't move.

He sat in a chair and wouldn't move.

I stood at the door of the jailhouse and tried to convince him too but he wouldn't come out.

I said, "Please dad. Please come out."

My mom said, "Come on Gary there's no sense in this. Just sign the ticket and let's go over to your mother's. She's expecting us."

But my dad wouldn't do anything.

He sat in a chair beside the cell and shook his head and said, "No. They're gonna put me in a cell and I'm not saying a damn thing. I'm expecting my first meal too. I know it's a law in this state that if you arrest someone you have to feed him."

So he sat beside the jail cell and listened to it all. He listened to Rip tell him it would be forgiven. He listened to the police officer tell him he didn't want to arrest him over a speeding ticket. He listened to mom ask him why. But he wouldn't come out because he knew it was not a jail, but his life. He knew he was going to stay there until the day he died.

MY DAD AT THE RACE

And then there was the time my dad got into it at the NASCAR race in Charlotte. For some reason we decided to go to the race and spend some time together—just the two of us. It was like one of those trips where your dad teaches you something or other, or he gives you some piece of wisdom.

We were coming out of the race after we watched the cars crash and smash and some guy poured beer on Earnhardt after he wrecked and Earnhardt tried to climb the fence and kick his ass.

"Damn guy trying to pour beer on Earnhardt," my dad said, distracted.

After the race was over we were walking alongside all of these drunks and all of these drunks were saying under their breath, "Holy shit I'm drunk," and then, "I'm so goddamn drunk I can't even see." Of course, these weren't even the real drunk people but the guys who were going to drive the real drunk people home.

I giggled at them and watched them and walked beside my dad. He just gave me a look like he always gave me when he didn't approve of someone's behavior and he didn't want me to laugh. We kept walking out of the racetrack and out into the parking lot and then out through this field and down a side road where we parked the Oldsmobile. My dad didn't believe in anything, but he believed in Oldsmobiles. He walked beside me and said, "Did you have fun?"

I tried to think of something to say but all I could come up with was "Yeah."

He put his hand on my shoulder, and we walked along.

Then all of a sudden Gary Mack took off running as fast as he could towards the Oldsmobile. I'd never seen him run before. He was fast. He wasn't normal fast—he was running back fast. I watched him run and shout, "Hey get off that car boy. That's a damn Oldsmobile."

At first I didn't even know what was going on, but then I saw the kid. It was this skinny kid with arms about as big around as broomsticks. He was drunk as hell. He was sitting on top of our car.

I ran behind my dad. The drunk kid was trying to get off the back of the car. The kid looked even younger when we got close up. He looked seventeen or sixteen. He was drunk and he was skinny and he had this scared look in his eyes and he was making this nervous sound in his throat like unnn unnn. Before I knew it Gary Mack was up in his face saying, "Boy, that's a good way to get your ass kicked."

The boy was still sitting on the car and said, "I'm…I'm…I'm sorry sir…I didn't mean any harm. I'm just from West Virginia too and wanted to write you a message and tell you I'm from West Virginia. That's all."

I looked and there was a half-finished note written with his finger on the dirty back window. It said: Hello I'm from WV too. My name is Michael. How are yo…

He didn't get the "you" finished though because there was some pissed off guy running towards him at full speed.

Now my dad said, "Well you don't mess with a man's automobile, boy."

The boy said more nervous, "Well I'm sorry. I'm sorry."

But before he could get down off of the car, my dad grabbed his arm and yanked the hell out of him, down onto the ground. The boy fell with a thud and it knocked the wind out of him: HUH.

It scared the kid and it scared me.

I said, "Dad."

But dad wouldn't listen to me. And the boy looked up scared and tried crawling away. Then the boy was shrieking nervous now like a pig eee eee, backing away into the darkness.

There were people standing around now and watching us. And so I just looked at my dad's face and he was a different man almost. We got back into the car and all around, the crowd was staring at us. My dad started the car and I leaned down into the backseat so no one could see me. As he drove away from the grassy field I looked up at the skinny boy's message that said, *Hello I'm from W.V too. My Name is Michael and I just wanted to say Hi. How are yo*. And so I sat there and imagined the last letter U. I imagined it inside my head and read the message over again as it glowed in the lights from the race track.

MY DAD

But my dad was more than that. We all are. There was one time we were taking a tour through Stonewall Jackson's home. There was this old fat woman with her two sons. There was our itty bitty tour guide taking us through the home when all of the sudden one of the sons just leaned over like he was going to pass out. The fat woman went, "Oh my God. What's wrong with him?"

The tour guide went, "Oh my God. What's wrong with him?"

Then they both went, "Oh my God. What's wrong with him?"

My dad walked past them and took the boy against his shoulder and didn't ask the boy a damn thing. Then he carried him down the stairs so the boy could go outside and get some fresh air.

And he was even more than that. He was more than the guy who scared the shit out of that kid at the race, and he was more than the guy who threw a possum further than any man had ever thrown a possum before. He whipped the possum around and around his head like it was a sling shot. Then he threw it high into the sky and the possum went up up up until it became a star. My dad was the guy from Kroger who worked in the produce department and whose whole job was making dead things look alive. He was the guy from Kroger who was always fighting rot. He was the one who sold groceries to all of the mothers in town.

And when I think of him now, I see all of my friends sprouting from the mountains like giants because he was the one who made the children grow.

MY MOM

And sometimes at night my mother sat up in bed with me and told stories. She told me about her Grandpa Ray who was a butcher in Beckley. And she told me how he left home when he was only sixteen years old and became a hobo. He rode all the way across the country and went hoboing for a couple of years and ended up in California, in Hollywood. After walking for a couple of days he wound up in a movie with a young Clark Gable. She didn't know if it was true or not or what the movie was, but he even had a line in the movie. It was a western and he came into the scene shouting to Clark Gable, "The injuns are coming. The injuns are coming."

One night years later I was with a girl I knew from school. I told her the story about Ray Smith, and we sat outside on these steps of an old building and I told her how I wanted to write stories someday. She told me if I ever wrote one to put in that line, "The injuns are coming." And no matter where she was she'd see that line and know I was talking to her. So here it is.

The injuns are coming.

Then my mom told me about her Grandpa Russ and how he was killed in a plane crash (and how years later Ray Smith married his wife). She told me he was a pilot. His wife had sent him out to the store to get a loaf of bread and some groceries. They think he must have met one of his pilot buddies at the store. They decided to go out to the airport and fly around a bit. And they don't know what happened really, but they think maybe Grandpa Russ had a heart attack when his buddy was in the back of the plane, and they just nosedived down into the ground. The plane crashed and they both died. And all that was left of him was a piece of his heel bone, some glass from the cockpit window, and his old watch with the hands of time burnt in it.

In the backseat of the car were a bag of groceries and a loaf of bread that never made it home.

Sometimes in the summer we went bear hunting. Bear hunting was really just walking on the mountain behind our house. And really it was my mother wanting to get some exercise, and knowing she was going to have to trick her child into coming along. She told me we were going bear hunting and she fixed me an egg sandwich, and we took off walking and hunting for bears.

But O God momma! I wonder what we would have done if we ever found one.

And then later that night my mother sat up in bed with me again and she told me about her uncle James. She told me how he died when he was a little boy. He'd just been to the world's fair in Chicago with his Boy Scout troop. Then one day that fall he was playing on the steps of this old building when a drunk guy and this woman came by. The boys started shouting at them, saying nasty things. The drunk threw a bottle at them and it hit James in the head. It killed him instantly.

My mother pointed to my temple and said, "It hit him right there in the temple."

It hit him right there.

I touched my temple where she was touching and hoped a drunk never threw a bottle and killed me.

My mother told me that later that evening they brought James' body back up to the house. Mom's grandpa Jim was sitting out on the porch. There was a whole crowd of people following the body as they carried it up to the house. So they put the body on the porch and grandma Dory cried a silent cry and threw herself on top of the body.

And then you could hear the cry and it was silent no more. So her husband reached up to the porch light so that no one could see and he twisted the light bulb off until it flick-flick-flickered and then finally went dark.

It wasn't until the next day that he looked down at his hand and all of the skin had been burnt off of his palm.

He didn't even realize it the night before.

His hand was a hand of fire.

His hand was a hand of burnt skin.

When we were on our bear hunting walk the next day my mother told me that it was never the same. And so Dory put all of her dead son's stuff into an old wooden chest. Each year during the spring she cleaned it out. She took out all of the stuff in the trunk and she cried and cried. She cried over her dead little boy's tie and she cried over the program to the Chicago World's Fair. And as each year passed she said she never stopped looking for his face. She never stopped believing that he escaped from the grave. She always thought he wasn't dead, but grown up. And he was living somewhere out there in the world, still alive.

And sometimes I used to sit out in the woods and just listen to the mountains. And sometimes I even imagined how the mountains became the mountains. I saw how the land used to be flat once and there was only the river and the giants. Then one day all of the giants grew tired and they decided to sit down and sleep. And they slept a sleep of a million years. The dirt and the rocks covered them up like graves and they were there now beneath the mountains. And one day they were going to wake and walk away and there would be no more mountains and we would be able to see past all of the hollers and the valleys and the rivers—all the way to the ocean.

And then on our bear hunting walk the next day, I told her that I wished my favorite episode of *Reading Rainbow* would come back on. A few months earlier, I had watched the episode with the dinosaur bones and I wanted to see it again. She told me that she talked to Levar Burton that very day and she asked him to play that episode again—just for me. So when I got home and turned on the TV... it was the *Reading Rainbow* episode where Levar Burton went searching for dinosaur bones.

I sat and watched the show and I said, "It's the dinosaur episode."

My mother said, "I told you."

And then she laughed and I thought that she was the most magical woman who ever lived.

CAPTAIN D'S

But if I had to tell you about my parents I'd probably tell you about a couple years ago when they went over to Beckley to eat at Captain D's. When they got there, they went inside, saying to each other like they always do, "You know what you're going to get?" And then, "Yeah I think I'm going to get that three piece fish dinner."

They stood in line and waited, and then they saw these two people standing in front of them. There was an old man carrying a Bible with a crocheted cover and there was his daughter who was probably in her forties and looked like she had something wrong with her. The old man told the girl behind the counter what he wanted and then he told his daughter, "Go ahead Janie. Go ahead and tell the woman what you want to eat."

The girl stood all nervous and pointed to the menu. "I'll have one of those." And the Captain D's girl turned around and said, "You mean a #1?"

And the girl said, "Yeah I want a #1."

My mom leaned over and whispered to my dad, "Gary, I don't think that girl can read."

My dad just nodded his head.

The Captain D's girl rang it all up and said, "That'll be 18.74 sir."

The old man looked into his wallet and slowly pulled out his check card. Then he handed it to the girl behind the counter.

She slid it through the register and then the register went beep.

So she tried it again and slid it through the register and the register went beep again.

So she handed the card back to the old man and said, "I'm sorry sir. Your card is denied." The old man reached out and his hands were shaking.

"What? It's denied."

His daughter said, "What's wrong Daddy? Why can't we eat?"

So the old man said, confused, "Well I just put some money in the bank the other day. I don't know."

Then the old man just repeated, "Well I put some money in there. I don't understand."

He started walking away and his daughter followed behind saying, "What's wrong Daddy? What's wrong?"

They walked out of the restaurant and started walking along together.

My parents ordered their food and paid for it with their coupons. They went to sit down. They sat and ate their three piece fish dinner and their hush puppies in silence. My dad ate his baked potato and they didn't say anything. They didn't say anything about the white-haired old man or his daughter who couldn't read. They didn't say a single word until my dad stopped eating and said, "Well I guess I should have given that man some money so they could eat."

My mom said, "I was thinking the same thing."

My dad said, "Well why didn't you say something to me?"

She looked out the window of the restaurant to see if she could still see them walking.

She looked as far as she could and said, "Well I don't see them. Do you think we might be able to catch them?"

So they got up and threw away their food and they left the Captain D's.

They got into the car and started driving. And they drove and they drove.

My dad said, "If he didn't put that money in on Friday it's hard to tell when they ate last time."

They kept driving down the road. They drove past the Go-Mart and they drove past the armory and they didn't see them. They drove back up the road and they still didn't see them. So they turned around and were starting to drive home when they passed a street and then up at the end of the street my mother saw something.

Was it them?

My dad turned down the street and went driving past the houses. Then the two figures grew closer.

And then they grew even closer.

My mom said, "It's them."

It was. It was the old man and his daughter walking together and holding the Bible. My dad stopped the car behind them.

My dad got out and said, "Hey buddy, I saw what happened to you back at Captain D's. And I just wanted to give you this so you could go and get something to eat." Then he reached into his wallet and pulled out a twenty dollar bill and handed it to the old man. The old man blushed and took the money. Then the old man's daughter raised her hands up into the sky and said, "Hallelujah. Hallelujah."

The old man said, "Yeah I don't know why that card didn't work. I don't know why."

My dad said, "Yeah sometimes it takes a couple of days."

The old man's daughter just kept shouting, "Praise Jesus. Praise his holy name. Praise him."

And then my dad said bye and got back into the car. And then my parents drove away. When my mother looked back in the mirror—the last thing she could see was the old man and his daughter, walking back to Captain D's so they could get something to eat.

THE FIRST TIME I MADE DIAMONDS

Sometimes when I was a boy I used to imagine that the coal was turning into diamonds…And one time I even tried making it happen. I heard my mother talking about it one day. A couple days later I took a chunk of coal and I dug a hole with an old rock. Then I put the coal into the ground and I thought, "Now all I have to do is wait a couple of days and I'll have some diamonds. Mom said all you have to do is wait a long time and it will happen." It was called time.

So I waited around for the next couple of days waiting for it to change. I played *Six Pack* with my neighbor Deborah. *Six Pack* is this crappy Kenny Rogers movie where he's a stock car driver. I was pretending to be Kenny Rogers and she was pretending to be the girl part. And I hated it because she always wanted to kiss me and she tasted like little girl spit. I took off and went out to my hole and started thinking about the diamonds and how I couldn't see them now, but how I could imagine them changing beneath the ground into shiny things.

After that a week went by, and I stood in front of the little hole I dug in the dirt pile and I took a big rock to use as a shovel. I thought for the umpteenth time about how everything changed. I told myself all I needed was time. I dug with the dirty rock and my face shined and the whole world did too. I dug and I dug, expecting to see the shiny thing. I dug one more time and there it was. But it wasn't a diamond. It was just a stupid chunk of coal. It was just a stupid chunk of dirty black coal. Shit.

I went all the way back home and I told my mother it didn't work.

She told me yes it does.

I told her about putting the coal into the ground and waiting for a couple of days.

So she laughed and said that a couple of days wasn't a long time, that it takes longer than that. She told me that sometimes you have to wait a million years.

And then she laughed again and said that a piece of coal was worth more than any stupid diamond. She giggled and repeated that five days wasn't a long time at all. But it was to me.

So I just closed my eyes and all I could see was blackness. I knew all we'd have to do was wait long enough and one day we'd come driving off of Sewell Mountain in some space ship and it would all be different. All we had to do was wait for a million years and one day we would return again in our spacesuits and it would all be there— just waiting for us. And it would all be shining.

KIDNEY STONES

I just wanted to be changed. I wanted to be changed more than anything in this world. That morning I was down at Rite Aid with my uncle Terry copying some of my grandma's old pictures when I felt this pain in my back. Of course, I didn't pay it any mind and just kept copying the picture of this old black and white shot of my grandfather from the late 30s.

It was one where he got in a fight with a police officer and they put him in jail.

It was a mugshot picture.

There was another picture of him somebody took a couple of years later, after he got religion.

He was sitting on the hood of a car, holding a Bible in his lap.

I stood and stared at the pictures and the pictures stared back. I thought about my grandfather who was a moonshiner once and then gave it all up to follow the Lord. I thought about Saul of Tarsus on the road to Damascus and being struck by a blinding light. He heard a voice and changed his name to Paul. That's how easy it was—you just had to change your name to Paul.

My uncle Terry put the picture of my grandfather Elgie holding the Bible on the picture scanner.

I giggled again because it was so stupid—the way it all sounded.

It all sounded so ridiculous really, how all of these visions were always about good and evil, God and the Devil.

We copied the Bible picture down and I started feeling this pain even more. I leaned over the counter hoping it would go away.

Go away. Go away.

But it didn't.

My uncle asked me in his strange hillbilly/New York/New Jersey/San Francisco accent, "You all right boy?"

So I smiled and said, "No I'm fine. I'm fine."

At first it came in waves, but then I was in pain.

"You need to go to the doctor boy?" he said again.

I shook my head no.

And so we finished up the pictures and I tried pretending I was fine.

I'm fine.

I'm fine.

Besides that I had to go to work that evening. I'd just luckily found a job a couple of weeks before and I couldn't lose it now.

But when I got home I could barely walk I was in so much pain.

I thought, "Oh shit, I think I'm having kidney stones."

So I sat around for another hour or so and took a whole handful of ibuprofen, hoping that would take care of it. But I needed to get going. I couldn't lose this job now. Things had been going so bad lately. I got into my car and started driving the hour it took to get to work and the pain was still surging in my back.

On the way there I thought about my grandfather and the road to Damascus.

"You're fine. You're fine."

But about halfway into the drive, I couldn't take it anymore.

I pulled over to this nasty little gas station and I went inside. My kidney stones were hurting me so much by this point, I had to bend over and start looking for a bathroom.

Picture this: A grown man bent over and searching desperately for a bathroom.

There was a pot-bellied woman working behind the counter who'd just finished checking in some deer this guy had killed, and there was an old man in there too spitting his Skoal spit into his Skoal cup and saying, "That Summer's County Bobcat defense sure is awesome this year. Might even take them to the playoffs."

He was smoking a cigarette too and holding it between his middle and ring fingers.

Spit. Smoke. Spit. Smoke.

I asked, "Where is your bathroom?" all out of breath and about ready to fall over. The old woman looked at me like I was some kind of meth-taking crazy man and pointed at the door towards the back.

"You got the shit pains don't you boy?" she said.

I smiled and shook my head like everything was okay and went into the bathroom all bent over and shut the door behind me. There wasn't a lock. There was a hole in the floor someone had stuffed a bunch of trash inside: cigarette packages, used tampons, candy wrappers, old newspapers.

"You're fine. You're fine," I kept saying to myself, and I could hear them talking outside.

I put my hand against the wall and I felt something stabbing me in the back. I breathed deep and the whole world went black.

I passed out.

The floor was cold and I dreamed my kidney stone dreams. I dreamed about the mugshot picture of my grandfather. I dreamed about my grandfather on the front of a car with a Bible on his lap, and a blinding light.

I dreamed about how he was a moonshiner once, and then he was a moonshiner no more.

And then I woke up.

I heard a voice outside the door saying, "Are you okay in there?"

I was still just sprawled on the floor. "Are you okay in there?" she said, trying to get the door open, but because I was passed out in front of it, the door wouldn't budge.

I cleared my throat and tried being as normal as possible. "Oh yeah I'm fine. Just give me a second. I think I'm just getting ready to pass a kidney stone."

Then the old woman said, "Well sonny, we don't allow people to pass kidney stones at the One Stop."

I didn't listen to her though.

I got up and unbuckled my pants and felt glass moving inside of me. Then I felt it moving through me and I passed it.

I SAW SOMETHING I COULDN'T BELIEVE.

I watched the kidney stone float in the toilet water and then sink.

THEN I HEARD SOMETHING I COULDN'T BELIEVE.

IT WAS A LOUD VOICE SHOUTING FROM HIGH ABOVE.

I COULDN'T EVEN TALK ABOUT IT.

The old woman said, "Do I need to call the law? I'll call the law if I have to."

"No I'm fine. I'm fine," I said, standing over the toilet. "Just give me a second."

I washed my face and walked outside.

They were all standing there and looking at me strange. It was like somebody didn't come in and pass out in the gas station bathroom every day.

I walked outside and I felt like everything was different now.

I felt like the old life was behind me.

I drove off to work and wondered if it really happened. I wondered if I saw what I saw and heard what I heard. And when I got to work I sat in the car for a few minutes before I went inside and asked myself, "Did that really happen? Did that…really…happen?"

When I went inside work I didn't tell anybody about the pain from the kidney stones on the way there. I didn't tell them about what had gone down.

And they didn't tell me about their pain either.

They didn't tell me about how their dads drank.

And the woman in the corner didn't tell me about how her husband cheated on her and she thought about killing herself.

The man in the front didn't tell me his mother died when he was eleven years old, and every day when he came home, he watched her die. He watched her die every day beside the television cartoons.

The other girl in the back didn't tell about how she was raped one night by this older guy when she was thirteen.

I didn't tell them about my pain either.

I didn't tell them about how Saul saw a blinding light on the road to Damascus and changed his name to Paul.

I didn't tell them about how everything changes in this world.

How could I?

How could I tell them about what happened to me in the bathroom on the way there?

How could I tell them about the blinding light, and how I passed a kidney stone shaped like a crucifix? How could I tell them about hearing a loud voice, shouting from on high, "Surely this is the TRUE Son of God in whom I'm well pleased. Arise now and awake the new prophet of the Lord."

And how can I tell you now what I know for sure?

How can I tell you now that my kingdom is at hand?

GO FORTH AND PREACH THIS GOSPEL CHILDREN.

HERNIA DOG

Who knows what his name was really? All I know is we used to call him Hernia Dog and he was always hanging around school, playing with the kids at recess time. We used to play with him too, running like hell out into the fields so we could play smear the queer and pinecone football. Hernia Dog was always right there, sitting all floppy-eared and young, with his hernia belly bouncing around. I guess it was a hernia. There was a growth of some kind hanging off of his side.

The girls in our class like Nicole and Ammie screamed for him to come play, and Hernia Dog chased after them too and listened as they gossiped about who was getting their periods and who liked who.

Then Hernia Dog watched the boys bloody each other's noses in our smear the queer fiascos. But the whole time—it was like he was different than other dogs. The whole time it was like he was one of us.

And now these were the days in the mountains when dogs were still not to be trusted. These were the days when packs of wild dogs still roamed the woods. It had been just a couple of weeks before that Nathan Adkins' little brother Nick was walking home and this pack of wild dogs jumped him and he almost died. One bit a big chunk out of his neck, and one bit his leg, and he just kicked and cried in his mother's arms until the ambulance came. He was a little guy in the 4th grade walking home from school one day and a pack of wild dogs almost ripped him to shreds. This is what happens sometimes in this crazy world.

Of course, these dogs were never caught. But Hernia Dog wasn't one of them. Hernia Dog was our friend. We knew he'd never join an outlaw dog gang and betray us, but what did we know about him.

What did we know about him when one day after school, I was walking back behind the football field with my friend Michael Chapman, and we saw Hernia Dog chained up to his dog house next to a porch? It was a half fallen down trailer/house with piles of dog turds all around it like little land mines. And there was a scary-looking guy working on a coal truck in the front yard. When Hernia Dog saw us he started whining a whine like, "Hey guys? I know you. Hey guys? You know me too."

But the scary looking guy working on the coal truck just walked over and yelled at him. Shut-up.

And so Hernia Dog shut up and we kept on walking.

A couple of days later somebody said something about Hernia Dog.

It was Randy Doogan and he started telling us about how he saw Hernia do something strange the day before.

He started telling about how Hernia Dog was sitting on top of his dog house, but then all of a sudden it looked like he was contemplating something.

He was trying to get his chain caught on purpose.

He was trying to get it caught.

He was trying to get it caught.

And then finally…the chain caught.

And just as it did—Hernia Dog walked to the side of the dog house and looked over like he was going to jump. The other dogs barked and yelped and started raising holy hell.

Yelp.

Yelp.

They were barking because Hernia Dog was getting ready to do something wrong.

So the scary-looking guy came over and grabbed him by the collar. He cussed and kicked Hernia Dog for being a damn coward who was thinking about trying to take his own life. And then he scolded him and said that suicides go to hell.

He told him it's better to suffer like the rest of us than have all of that pain go away.

But Randy swore it was true.

We all laughed at how ridiculous his story was.

But of course we were in junior high now. We didn't really see

Hernia Dog anymore. Every now and then he'd get loose.

And we'd see him outside the school, waiting for us to come outside.

But now when we came outside to change classes or go to football practice, we didn't run and call his name and tickle his bulge like before. We just walked on by and he'd follow behind us—wondering what went wrong.

Something always goes wrong, doesn't it?

And so it seemed like years passed before we ever saw him again. It was the night of the 9th grade dance and I was there with my girl Jamie who I used to have brilliant conversations with, like…

What are you doing?

Nothing.

What are you doing?

Nothing.

Silence for awhile.

Okay.

Bye.

Okay.

Bye.

So here we were together.

And everybody else was getting ready to dance.

You know the kind?

It's the kind of dance where the guy puts his hands on the girl's hips, and then the girl puts her arms around the guy's neck. And then they move back and forth, back and forth until the song finally ends. Then the next song begins.

And then you're trying to sneak off…to go do…you know what?…to go find hidden skin in the dark.

And so that night we were hanging around the gymnasium which was about ready to fall in. We were all standing around before we went inside. A couple of the guys were chewing and spitting spit into their styrofoam spit cups stuffed full of paper towels.

A couple of the girls were smoking cigarettes behind the pine trees—Nicole and Ammie. They were smoking something at least. I turned around and I saw him. It was Hernia Dog.

He looked so different now.

He looked so old.

"Ah shit—that dog's still alive?" Randy said.

All the girls went, "Oh he looks so pitiful."

But nobody tried petting him because of his nasty looking hernia.

And nobody wanted to touch him because he smelled so bad.

It looked like his fur was missing in patches too like he'd been burned.

"Oh God he smells so horrible," one of the girls finally said. "He smells like he has cancer."

And he did.

Everyone held their noses and Randy tried kicking him away, "Get the fuck out of here you old dog. Git."

The dog ran a few steps, but he wouldn't move. Darren tried spitting tobacco juice at him, but he just sat there.

The girls went, "Oh don't. He's just an old dog."

Randy said, "Well I'm sorry. He just smells so bad."

Then he stomped at him. But Hernia just sat and looked at us.

He wouldn't move and it was like he wanted to tell us something, like he was trying to say goodbye.

And so I forgot about him. It had been years, and we were hanging around the Handy Place. We were all grownups now. I guess that's what you'd call it. We were talking to Darren who had just got this girl pregnant. He was talking about how they didn't have enough money to get rid of it.

Then out of nowhere Randy said, "Oh shit, I almost forgot."

And then we were all quiet.

"You know that old dog with the hernia that used to hang around school?"

We all nodded our heads, "Yes."

Then he said, "Well I swear to shit he finally did it. He finally did it."

And now we listened.

We listened as Randy told us about how Hernia Dog had escaped from his chains.

And Randy saw him standing alongside the road.

And so Randy waved at Hernia Dog.

Wave.

But Hernia Dog just looked at him sad, like he was waiting on something.

Then Randy saw it coming. He saw what Hernia Dog was waiting on.

It was a coal truck, rolling up Route 60 at 60 MPH.

It was like Hernia Dog had been waiting just for this.

It was like he'd been waiting just for this all of these years.

And then—AHHHH.

So Hernia Dog took off running straight at the coal truck, running as fast as he could.

The coal truck stomped on its horn….errrrrrrrrrrrrr………..but Hernia Dog just kept charging at it….straight for it…straight for it…

And so somebody tried to laugh. And then somebody shook their head like it wasn't true. But then they stopped because we knew it was true. I stood and tried imagining it all. I thought about my childhood and I imagined Hernia Dog for one last time running straight at the coal truck.

Then I heard a coal truck from somewhere far away and it was honking its horn for us.

Can you hear it?

THIS IS A STORY WITH A PHONE NUMBER IN IT

I don't know if you've ever been a telemarketer before, but I have. I used to make call after call, working at this telemarketing place in Huntington, WV.

Hello my name is Scott McClanahan for the West Virginia Fraternal Order of Police.

Click.

Hello my name is Scott McClanahan for the Fraternal Order of Police.

Click.

Hello my name is Scott McClanahan for.

Click.

Hello my name is.

Click.

And you always had to do it in this deep voice so you could fool people into thinking you were a real state trooper, and not just some punk-ass kid.

The first day I worked there, I sat next to this guy named Matt. He was this older guy, probably about forty-five or fifty years old, and he had a family of four. He supported them on his seven dollars an hour. He was just this aww shucks guy, but once he got on the phone he was badass. One day I was sitting beside him as he shouted at this poor old woman, "You will give LADY. My best friend was killed in the line of duty last year. You WILL GIVE!"

Of course, we were just pretending to be police officers.

She finally ended up giving 150 dollars.

And he had all kinds of tricks too, like shouting, "Hey Sarge. I'll see you out at the range in about 15 minutes."

Then during the next phone call, he even started talking in this strange accent and the person gave him 75 dollars.

He looked over and said, "That's why they call me the best."

Then B-Dawg, the manager, shouted, "And tonight's top caller and winner of 100 dollars is you know who? Matt."

Then later that evening on our break, Matt said, "Yeah I always take the family to a nice restaurant each week on this. We always go to Wendy's on Saturday night and have a good time."

He meant this with no irony whatsoever.

Wendy's was a nice restaurant to him.

When we got back from break I kept on calling. "Hello my name is Scott McClanahan with the West Virginia Fraternal Order of Police."

On the other end there was this asshole from a rich neighborhood in California. He was shouting, "Hey you shit ass. What are you making, like minimum wage? I want to know how much of this goes to the police?"

I started my rebuttal, "Well sir because of the high costs of production."

He cut me off.

"Yeah only about 5 percent goes," he said like he read it in a newspaper story somewhere. "This is nothing but a scam. I know what you guys are doing."

Matt just smiled like a kind father, pointed to my keyboard, and said, "Hit that button." That button was F-4.

I hit F-4 and asked what it would do?

He said, "It'll call him back every five minutes for the next five hours."

And that's just what happened.

Ring.

Ring.

Ring.

The dumb fucker didn't even take the phone off the hook, but answered each time cussing and carrying on and getting ready to have a heart attack as his number bounced from caller to caller throughout the office.

Over the next couple of weeks I tried telling people about how wonderful it was being a telemarketer. I tried telling people how strange it was to sit calling somebody all the way across the country even though here I was in little piss ant WV. And when they picked up the phone, I was always taught to say their first name. This was so they'd think I was someone who knew them.

I said, "Hey Jerry" and a little girl voice said, "No, do you want to talk with him?"

"Sure."

"May I ask who is calling?"

"It's Scott McClanahan."

And then on the other end I heard this little girl voice that said, "DAAADDD? Scott McClanahan's calling."

And here I was having my name shouted a thousand miles away.

Sometimes I wondered if I'd ever come across another Scott McClanahan age 21 in another part of the country. And maybe we were the same person, but we were living different realities. If I ever met myself I wondered...

What would he say?

What would I say?

Would he give me money?

Now these were the type of things I thought about walking home at night through the dark alleys of Huntington, even though friends told me it was a bad idea and I should walk the main road. I walked slow through the evening dark and passed women standing around smoking cigarettes.

"Hey," one said all sexy like she knew me.

"Hey," I said. I thought, "What a nice woman."

I never had such a pretty woman dressed in sexy clothes come right out and say "Hi" to me.

Maybe she thought I was cute.

It made me feel good about myself.

After a couple of months of calling people it started wearing on me. We had to meet quotas each week at the telemarketing place and even though I was a top level caller, I was running into some bad luck.

Hello my name is...

Click.

Hello my name is Scott McClanahan.

Click.

There were other things too. The name of the company changed every other week, paychecks were late a week at a time, and one guy was constantly listening to a police scanner. I guess if the cops were coming they could get the massive call computers out the door and down the freight elevators before the coppers showed up.

I was having such bad luck calling one night I even told one of the managers that I was sorry, but my girlfriends' mother had died the day before and I just wasn't myself.

She didn't die.

I mean I was lying now.

I was a liar.

So when I came home that night Kim was all over me.

"I mean why would you say my mom died?"

"I know. I know. I panicked. I thought they were going to fire me."

"Fire you? Scott, it's a telemarketer job that pays $7.00 an hour. Most people are there to earn money so they can get high. I mean they have work release prisoners working there. Besides that, you hate it. So why don't you just quit?"

I was thinking about it. I was tired of walking home through the dark and beating people out of money and them not knowing where it was going. I was tired of waving at the women in the pretty clothes and wanting them to wave back. So I made a plan to leave, but then the next night my luck started changing.

I started going "Hello" and before I could even get it out they gave me 75 dollars.

"Hello my name is Scott McClanahan…"and the caller gave me 150.

"Hello my name is…" and they gave me 25.

And so I sent out at least three or four info packets for future donations.

I was in the zone.

Matt even gave me a high five.

And then B-Dawg threw me a t-shirt because I was the top caller for the night, "Hell yeah."

Maybe I wasn't quitting.

But then it happened. The phone clicked and the info popped into my computer screen—65 years old. White male. Georgia. He gave 30 dollars last year.

"Hello," he said real quiet on the other end. And so I went through my whole spiel.

I told him about the FOP.

I told him thanks for his past support.

I asked him if the FOP could count on him again this year.

It was quiet again.

And then he finally said, "Well sir, I'm sorry......I'd really like to......But I just don't know if I can."

I immediately went into my first rebuttal.

"Well sir we appreciate your past support of 30 dollars but please realize..."

And then he said, "No, no. I understand what you're saying...... I always love to help out the troopers, but I don't know if I can."

And then there was silence.

Then he said, "I lost my daughter...three days ago...in a car crash."

And so I started looking through my rebuttals, but I didn't have one for a guy who had lost his daughter in a car wreck.

I just said, "Oh I'm sorry sir."

And he started talking so that I couldn't even say anything else. "From what we can tell the road was wet and she was going too fast."

Then he was quiet and said, "They said she lost control and wrecked...she died."

And then it was quiet again and I could hear something else. I could hear him crying on the other end.

I improvised, "Well sir I'm sorry to hear about your loss but maybe our 25 dollar level would make you feel better as a donation to the FOP in your daughter's memory."

He said, "But that's just the thing. I don't know."

So I looked over at the manager B-Dawg and he was running his finger across his throat—in a throat slash motion which meant, "Cut the phone call. Cut it."

I said quick, "Well sir why don't I just send you an info packet and you can make the decision yourself? Okay?"

But he wouldn't have any of it.

He whispered, "No, don't go. Please don't go. It's good to talk to someone. I've just been stuck in this house and I'm so lonely. Please don't go. I'm so lonely."

And I didn't say anything

Then I heard CLICK.

The call was cut.

I looked over at Brian, the manager, and he had cut the call himself. He walked over to me and said, "I'm sorry you had one of those fucking criers. Shit, sometimes those old fuckers just talk and talk and talk for hours about how this happened to this person and how that happened to this person."

And then he said how sometimes you can talk for ten minutes and they won't give you a nickel. "Lonely people babbling."

Then the next call started ringing into my computer and I went back to work saying, "Hello my name is Scott McClanahan."

"Hello my name is Scott McClanahan."

"Hello my name is Scott McClanahan."

"Hello my name is Scott McClanahan."

And so that night I walked home passing the sexy girl in the alley who was smoking cigarettes. And for some reason this time she didn't look pretty anymore. She looked cut up and scared and her eyes looked like werewolf eyes. I still tried waving "Hi" at her like a big dork. I still thought it was strange you didn't say hello to people in a city when you passed them.

Why is that?

And the woman didn't even look at me but just kept her head down and turned away like I was a werewolf too. And so I walked all the way back to my apartment watching the lights from the cars zipping down 3rd Avenue like stars. So I unlocked the door, and locked it behind me and I sat down beside the telephone in my tiny apartment, hoping the phone would ring—just like hopefully somebody will call 304-252-0430 right now, and then maybe I won't be so lonely anymore.

THE COUPLE

I didn't have any money for dinner. I'd never even been on a date before—or at least a *date* date. When I was in school it was all about hooking up at parties and hanging out together with a whole group of friends and maybe finding each other later that night. But this was like a real date. At least it felt like a real date when I called her up that morning and asked her if she wanted to go up to Pipestem State Park and look out over the mountains. I told her I didn't have any money for dinner, but she didn't seem to mind, or at least she thought I was joking. So that afternoon I picked her up and drove out to Pipestem. Once we got there, we walked hand in hand, up to the observation tower, and she started telling me about how she used to have a lazy eye when she was a kid. It was so bad she even had to wear an eye patch in order to correct it, and all the kids at school started calling her "the pirate."

She laughed.

And then we both laughed at how ridiculous the whole world was.

We kept right on laughing and started climbing the steps of the observation tower, counting them on the way up—1, 2, 3, 4, 5, 6, 10, 20, 30, 40. Then after about eighty we finally got up to the top and caught our breath. It was beautiful up there. We laughed some more and I told her what a lucky girl she was being on such an expensive date and if she played her cards right I had a whole pocketful of coupons for the Pizza Hut lunch buffet. If we scraped together our nickels and dimes then maybe we could go. She laughed again and I noticed she had a cracked front tooth, which looked so cute when she grinned. We stood looking out over the mountains.

I held her hand and we didn't laugh anymore.

I pointed at the mountains and told her how they were formed.

I told her how the mountains weren't created by the last ice age really, but were created by water runoff from the last ice age. So she stood and smiled. And then she told me how boring that story was. I kissed her and tasted the taste of chewing gum on her chewing gum tasting lips.

But then we noticed this other couple walking up to the observation tower from below. It was a guy and a girl. They counted their steps on the way up too—1, 2, 3, 4, 5, 6, 10, 20, 30, 40.

It was this old guy who looked like he was about forty and he had a trach scar. He was with this pretty girl who couldn't have been any more than twenty. They were the type of couple that makes you think, what the hell is that girl doing with that guy?

They were holding hands and they had a pizza and a two liter bottle of pop and a picnic basket full of picnic stuff.

FOOD!

They giggled all out of breath when they got to the top of the tower just like we had.

Then they noticed us and nodded their heads "hello."

"Hello."

We grinned and nodded our heads "hello" back.

"Hello."

Then we went right back to talking, as they set up all of their picnic stuff on the other side like they were boyfriend and girlfriend. They had paper plates, and paper cups, and diet pop, and pizza.

We stood on the other side listening to them.

Kim said, "That pizza smells good. I'm getting hungry."

But I didn't say anything about it, wondering if she really thought I was just joking about us not going to dinner. I wasn't joking though. I really wasn't.

Then I saw something.

What was that?

I saw something moving in the woods beneath us. I saw this woman walking out of the woods towards the observation tower. She was wearing mom clothes and she had a mom haircut.

She was screaming something, coming closer to us, but I couldn't make it out.

WHAT?

She screamed again and this time it sounded shotgun loud.

She shouted, "Steven. Steven. You cheating motherfucker. Get your ass down here right now."

And so Steven, the cheating motherfucker, just sat over his pizza and didn't know what to do.

He dropped his head like he was praying about it.

My stomach dropped.

Kim looked nervous.

It was Steven's wife.

And the wife had two little boys with her too, dragging them behind her like dirty sheets.

The little boys were crying, "Mommy, Mommy."

The pretty girl Steven was with looked like she didn't know what to do. It was like she didn't even know he was married.

Who knows?

Finally Steven got up and walked down the steps of the observation tower 80, 70, 60, 50, 40, 10, 9, 8, 7, 6, saying with a quiet voice on the way, "Ah honey. We haven't done nothing. We were just talking and eating some pizza."

But his wife stood at the bottom of the stairs holding the little fists of their two little confused kids.

She screamed, "HOW dare you—you stupid asshole." Then she whispered all pathetic, "You told me it was over. You told me it was finished."

And so Kim stood there scared and said, "Scott. I think we should leave. This is none of our business. We need to get out of here."

I giggled, "Ah no. It's all right."

Then we watched Steven's pretty friend walk all the way down to the bottom of the steps. She was nervous and scared too.

His wife started screaming at her, "You little bitch whore. You want to introduce yourself to your fucking boyfriend's wife and kids."

Then Steven said, "Honey she's not a whore. She's just a friend."

And then there was something else moving in the trees.

It was an old guy who I took to be Steven's father-in-law, and a muscular and bearded guy, who I took to be Steven's brother-in-law.

It was Steven's in-laws.

Slowly they walked over to where the wife was screaming and kicking and kicking and crying. And then Steven held out his hand to the father-in-law and the brother-in-law too, but instead of shaking his hand—they jumped on him. The brother-in-law got a hold of

Steven's arms and then he threw Steven on the ground. Then he was on top of Steven punching him in the face and the father-in-law just stood by watching.

The father-in-law was smoking a cigarette and after a while he started kicking Steven in the side.

He kicked soft.

Then he puffed his cigarette. Puff.

Then he kicked again.

Then he puffed his cigarette. Puff.

Then he kicked again.

I guess Steven had been warned about this type of behavior before.

"Scott. I think we should get out of here," Kim said. "What if they have a gun?"

I just giggled and said, "Ah no. Settle down. You watch too much TV. They're just gonna kick his ass a little bit."

So the wife started chasing the young girl towards the woods so she could beat the shit out of her, shouting "You little bitch. You little bitch. I'm gonna beat the shit out of you."

The two little kids sat in the grass watching it all.

And then I saw it.

Pizza.

I pointed over to the pizza and it was sitting there all alone and delicious.

I giggled and rubbed my belly like I was hungry.

Kim looked at me…

"Oh no," she said. "Oh no. We can't."

But I held her hand and walked over to where the pizza was.

She kept saying, "No. No."

I picked up the two liter and poured some pop out in the paper cups.

I handed it to her saying in my best cockney accent, "Me lady."

"Scott what are we doing?" she said.

I handed her a piece of pizza and I took a piece of pizza too.

I said, "Oh don't worry. We're just gonna watch the show."

And so we watched the wife dressed in her mom haircut and dressed in her mom clothes chasing the girl into the woods before the girl finally fell. The wife smacked her in the side of the head. Then she started ripping out a clump of the girl's hair, until a big clump came out.

Ah hell.

It was a hair extension.

And then the wife smacked the girl a couple more times before walking back and screaming at Steven who was now held in a head lock, "Steven I swear to God. I'm getting a divorce and you'll never see these kids. You'll never see these babies again. You'll never see these babies."

Kim and I sat eating the pizza and it felt so wrong to watch it all. We watched one of the little boys on his knees digging in the dirt with an old stick. Mommy was crying, and Daddy was crying and bleeding, and Mommy's daddy and Mommy's brother were crying and punching. The little boys were on their knees acting like this wasn't happening. They looked like the whole world was invisible almost. They acted like they were invisible too.

And so we looked at each other.

We watched the brother-in-law whack Steven with one more kidney punch before finally getting off. Steven was coughing up blood now.

And then the brother-in-law got up and started walking away with his father who was still smoking on his cigarette. Puff. Puff.

The wife was gone too, but we could hear her cries from far away. It sounded like an animal dying.

After five minutes Steven finally sat up on all fours and started spitting out more blood.

His face was all swollen up like a rotten watermelon.

He kept putting his fingers to his lips like he was trying to see if he was still bleeding.

Fingers.

Blood.

Fingers.

Blood.

Yep, he was still bleeding.

And so Kim and I sat and ate their pizza and we drank their pop and we watched it all because this wasn't our life being destroyed. We looked at the invisible little boys and they looked at us, and now we all wanted to be invisible too.

THE LAST TIME I STOLE
WALT WHITMAN'S SOLE

I've stolen things before. I've stolen a chestnut from Kroger when I was four, and some bubblegum from a store when I was twelve. I ripped out a couple of pages from the *Joy of Sex* when I was fourteen and stuffed them in my pockets for a secret time later on. I've stolen the *Collected Works of Nathanael West* and the *Bhagavad-Gita* from a used bookstore when I was nineteen.

But it wasn't until just a couple of years ago that I ever tried stealing something as a grown man. It started when Kim asked me to go home with her for Thanksgiving. She lived in the same town Walt Whitman was from, and there was a Walt Whitman birthplace and historic site we could visit. I decided to go.

Of course, I should have known something was wrong when she insisted we listen to the *Grease* soundtrack all the way there. If there's one thing that unites all girls from Long Island it's the *Grease* soundtrack and a profound interest in weight loss. Kim made me sing all of the John Travolta parts even though I hated it. *I got chills they're multiplying—it's electrifying.*

I should have known something else was wrong when she said, "Now we're going to stay with my mom, but I'm just warning you. If she starts talking about her spirit animal or healing your pain body, don't think anything about it. My mom is a witch."

Of course, I didn't say anything about it. But just a couple of minutes after we got there, Kim's mom just looked over at me and said, "So tell me Scott. What's your spirit animal?"

She told me her spirit animal was the raven and she could heal people just by placing her hands on them. She was a healer and a caster of spells. I sat in a chair and kept quiet. Then I felt this presence behind me. I felt these hands, hovering just a few inches from the top of my head. I turned around surprised. Shit.

It was Kim's mom standing there. She had her eyes closed and her arms out. She was wearing a black gown now.

"You're not doing that weird healing shit on Scott are you?" Kim asked from the bathroom. She was getting ready so we could go to dinner later that evening with her dad.

Kim's mom opened her eyes reeealllll slow and said, "Oh no sweetie. I would never do that. I would never do any unsolicited healings. However, the energy tells me that he's looking for someone."

Walt Whitman.

Of course, I should have known the trip wasn't getting any better when we sat down with Kim's dad that night at this fancy Italian restaurant and he proceeded to order a drink. He was this little red-faced, Billy Joel looking Irish guy. He didn't really say anything to me except something about how if I ever hurt his daughter, "Maggots would eat out my eyeballs."

Then he ordered another drink.

I told Kim, "Your father really is a charming man. He's really making me feel very welcome here."

Her dad finished up that drink and then he ordered another. He finished up that drink and then he ordered another. I didn't know if seeing some dead poet's birthplace was worth this. I knew it wasn't worth it when her father was brought the bill and he completely freaked out.

At first it was just him cussing beneath his breath, but then I looked over and he was taking out his lighter, and then he was waving the lighter around and around his head and he was shouting at the top of his lungs, "I'm gonna burn this guinea joint down. I'm gonna burn this fucking guinea joint down."

Kim said, "Do something Scott."

I was so shocked I just stood there.

I thought, "Guineas? What type of person is racist against Italians in this day and age?" Besides that, most of the guys working in this joint were just young Mexican men pretending to be Italians.

But I didn't say anything.

I kept saying to myself, "It's gonna get better. It's gonna get better."

At least that's what I kept repeating the next morning when we got up and drove over for what I'd come here for. On the way over there, we passed the Walt Whitman Mall. The Walt Whitman Mall? Then we finally came to this little wooded area and a historic marker that said, "Walt Whitman Birthplace and Historic Site."

We got out and walked into the visitor center and this 40ish looking lady behind the counter said, "May I help you?" I said, "Yes mam. I think you can. We're wanting to go on a tour."

The woman looked at me and said, "Oh you're not from around here are you?"

I said just like every time this happens, "No mam. I'm from West Virginia."

Then she asked, "Now what part of Virginia are you from?"

I explained, "No mam, I'm from West Virginia. It's a real state."

Then I asked her how much tickets were and she said, "Oh I'm sorry, but we're closed to the public today."

What?

And just about that time—a school bus pulled up outside. A bunch of smartass-looking 8th graders walked off the bus, through the door, past me and out the door, where a tour guide was already waiting on them.

The tour guide shouted above their voices, "Walt Whitman was born on this site on May 31, 1819. He was a poet, a journalist, and a true lover of freedom."

Kim said, "I thought you were closed to the public?"

The woman told us they were always closed to the public on the third Monday of every month and allowed local school groups to come by.

I told her that we could go with the school group on a tour, we didn't mind.

But she just shook her head and said she was sorry, the third Monday was always reserved for school groups. It was the rule.

Kim patted my shoulder and said, "It's all right, we can just come back tomorrow."

But the woman just shook her head again and said she was sorry but they were closed tomorrow too. On the third Tuesday of every month they were closed for cleaning purposes.

It was the rule.

What? We had to leave the next day. We wouldn't be able to go.

Kim tried cheering me up. Later that night she took me to a party at one of her friends. And when we walked in, I knew the trip wasn't getting any better. I listened to the music playing in the background, *I got chills they're multiplying. It's electrifying.*

Kim laughed and told me I should sing along and show her friends my great Travolta voice.

Her friends went, "Yeah Scott, do it, do it. Do it for us."

But I refused. They wouldn't appreciate my Travolta voice. After I drank a couple of beers though, I did sing a couple of lines from the Olivia Newton John part. *Well you better shape up/cause I need a man/and my heart is set on you.* I started feeling better, but then one of Kim's friends started telling me about how one of their overweight friends from childhood was battling cancer now.

She said, "I saw her recently and she's lost a lot of weight."

I said, "Well I guess cancer is not all that bad is it? At least she's losing weight."

And instead of laughing she just shook her head like this was true. "I know. I know." Then she asked me why I was here and looked so sad.

I told her I wanted to see Walt Whitman, but it was closed.

The girl looked at me confused, "No. It's not. The Walt Whitman Mall doesn't close until like 10 at night."

I said, "No, I mean the Walt Whitman birthplace. The poet? You know where he was born?"

"Oh," the girl said. "I didn't know he was a real person. I just thought that was the name of the mall."

So I smiled. I smiled and I heard these lines. *If you want me again look for me under your boot soles. Failing to find me at first keep encouraged/missing me one place search another/I stop somewhere waiting for you.*

I listened to Whitman's words and I looked out from the window and all I could see was one thing through all of the trees.

It was the Walt Whitman Mall.

It shined in the darkness now and I knew what I had to do. I had to steal a copy of Walt Whitman's *Leaves of Grass* from the Walt Whitman Mall the next morning.

The next morning I didn't even say anything about my plan to Kim. I waited for her and her mom to leave so they could go see her grandma. I told Kim I was going to take the car and fill it up with gas. I was Okay.

I didn't know the way really but I felt something was guiding me. I felt something was guiding me when I saw it appear in front of me like a temple—the Walt Whitman Mall.

I felt something guiding me as I parked the car. It was so early there weren't any people inside. I found the bookstore on the mall map and kept thinking about the only rule I knew about shoplifting.

The rule: If anyone catches you, run like hell.

So I walked down the empty mall and went inside the bookstore. There was a mousy looking girl working behind the counter, and she didn't even look like she was awake. I didn't even know what I was going to do with the book after I stole it. Of course, the bookstore girl was drinking coffee and typing stuff into the computer. There was a part of me going, "What are you doing Scott? What are you doing? What the fuck are you doing?"

But I didn't stop.

I just walked to the literature section and I scanned the W section. Wilde, Wolfe, Woolf.

No Whitman.

So I scanned again, Wilde, Wolfe, Woolf, and Richard Wright's *Black Boy.*

No Whitman.

So I went over to the fiction section thinking someone had put it there by mistake. I scanned the shelf—Wouk, Tom Wolfe, Alice Walker.

No Whitman.

Wouk, Wolfe, Alice Walker.

I scanned again. Whitman? Whitman? No Whitman.

I walked over to the counter and the girl working behind it asked, "May I help you find anything, sir?"

Of course, I knew asking her a question and having her notice me was going to make this a lot riskier.

I kept saying inside my head, "Just leave Scott. Just leave. What are you doing?"

But I said it anyway, "Yes, I am looking for a copy of Walt Whitman's *Leaves of Grass.*" She didn't say anything but typed it into the computer. It was like she couldn't speak without the computer screen telling her what to say.

The computer screen blinked a new screen and then she said, "Oh I'm sorry, we don't have it in stock for some reason. But we might be able to order a copy for you."

I just shook my head "no" and heard a voice inside my head. *Look for me under your boot soles/I stop somewhere waiting for you.*

And so I turned away and drifted back to the literature section: Wilde, Wolfe, Woolf.

No Whitman.

Wilde, Wolfe, Woolf, Richard Wright.

No Whitman.

He wasn't there.

And then it was like I was lost in some strange spell, a strange spell cast over me by a WITCH. This was a witch who wasn't good or bad. I looked back at the counter where the book girl was and she wasn't there anymore.

All I could see were books. There were books about all of the people I knew. I took a couple of them off the shelf, but they were all written in these strange languages that I didn't recognize.

Imagine: Books telling the future stories of all the people in our lives.

And so that's when I saw it. It was a book called *The Life and Death of Scott McClanahan.* It was such a slim volume. It worried me, but when I opened it up there were only blank pages—all blank pages except for the last page. On the last page was a poem written by Walt Whitman but signed with my name, a poem stolen by Scott McClanahan.

You will hardly know who I am or what I mean
But I shall bring you sickness and loneliness nonetheless.
If you want me again look for me
Under your Nikes

Failing to fetch me at first give up
Missing me one place go home
You're a Goddamn stranger here.

I stop nowhere waiting for you

But I am always out there

—running…
—running…

And then there was a muzak song drifting inside my head. It was like a whisper song and I was singing along.

You're the one that I want
You are the one I want
Woo hoo woo hoo
Honey

The one that I want
You are the one I want
Woo hoo woo hoo
Honey

And so I fucking ran.

THE PRISONERS

I used to teach this class at the federal prison in Beckley, WV. On the first day I called up education from the phone at the main desk. I was so nervous and fifteen minutes later the prison guard, Kincaid, showed up. He was walking towards me, all sawed off and with these big linebacker arms. He searched me and had me take off my shoes and put them back on.

He said, "My name's Kincaid and I'll give you a piece of advice. You can't trust anybody in here."

He took my keys and left them at the control desk saying, "We keep your car keys so if there is ever a hostage situation, they can't put a gun to your head and have you drive them off the premises."

I couldn't tell if he was joking.

He took me inside the prison and it took fifteen minutes just to go through six or seven locked doors, which crashed like cars when they opened and closed.

SMASH.

SMASH.

We walked along and he told me sometimes guys will get in fights just so they can go to solitary, and if I noticed anything in my class to let him know.

He said, "I guess they pick up some morphine or heroin along the way and they like going to solitary so they can shove it up their ass and enjoy it in privacy."

I finally just stood there thinking, "I don't think this guy is joking."

I was already paranoid from a report I read the week before on the Columbian drug cartels sending hit lists through written code. I was worried the guys would put these hidden messages in their essays ordering the death of someone on the outside. I imagined drug cartel guys breaking into my office to steal the essays and get the codes.

But then I stopped thinking because Kincaid gave me a radio.

He pointed to a red button on the top of it and said, "Now if anyone's ever attacking you, just hit this red button and it will probably save your life."

But then he just laughed and said, "Unfortunately this one is broken, so the red button doesn't work, but I'll try to get one for you next week. So if anybody tries to kill you this week, we're screwed."

Was this a joke?

And then we both just laughed, nervous.

Was this joking?

We started walking again.

We walked through a locked door and then another and then another.

But once I got inside the prison's education department, which only consisted of about one hundred Bibles dropped off by local churches, everything was fine.

I *did* make the mistake of introducing myself to the guys as Scott. When Kincaid walked by the room and heard them calling me this, he knocked on the glass and stuck his head inside the door shouting like an asshole cop, "Hey guys, you call him Mr. McClanahan."

I apologized, I'm sorry, I'm sorry, and then he left, but not before making one of the prisoners remove a fro pick.

I heard one of the guys saying, "Damn that guy is wound about two wounds too tight." And then another guy said, "You have to be a sick motherfucker to make the choice to come inside a prison."

Then someone else said, "At least he gets paid to be here—about $65,000 from what I hear."

Then another guy said, "Yeah $65,000 of hell."

I reminded them I was choosing to be here and I was only a volunteer from a local community college.

Everybody laughed like that was the sickest joke of all.

I was a dumb bastard all right.

I calmed everybody down and started taking roll by the list of prisoners provided by the prison. I read the list of students on my list of inmates (no first names), but just Inmate 1118046 D. Johnson.

Inmate 1190647 E. Johnson.

Inmate 1117843 T. Johnson.

I tried to make a joke, saying, "Man the world's been rough on you Johnson boys this year."

Nobody laughed.

I had them go around and introduce themselves—inmate 118046 D. Johnson. "Man I just want to get my life together. I've made some mistakes and I just want to get out and become a better member of society."

Inmate 119847 E. Johnson. "Man I just want to get my life together. I've made some mistakes and I just want to get out and become a better member of society."

Inmate 1117843. "Man I just want to…"

You get the point.

It was like this story after story until all the way down at the end of the list was inmate 117486 R. Rodriguez.

I knew before he even spoke—he was different.

He was different because there was laughter and life inside his eyes.

He said, "Man y'all a bunch of fools."

He said, "When I get out I just want to get me some motherfucking ho's and some motherfucking weed. And I'm not gonna do anything except sit around all day and smoke sweet weed and fuck pussy."

And so everybody laughed and then one of them said, "You going back to selling?"

Rodriguez said, "Hell yes. I'll know how much I can carry on me without it being a felony now."

Everybody laughed some more. I knew he was different.

I knew he was different because he wasn't like the rest of us. Rodriguez was a rare breed. Rodriguez was a truth teller.

I knew he was different that next week after I had them read an essay by George Orwell called "Shooting an Elephant."

I asked whether or not Orwell was right in shooting the elephant.

One of the guys named Smoot, who was this big, muscular, skinhead guy said, "I think that Orwell's nothing but a punk-ass bitch. He reminds me of some of them snitch bitches around here. I've been in gladiator schools and he wouldn't last in gladiator schools."

By then Rodriguez just smiled at me and he started to calm Smoot down. It's all right. It's all right.

And then Rodriguez smiled some more and started talking about the difference between free will and whether we're conditioned to behave in a certain way. He talked about how we really don't know one another—especially ourselves. He talked about how Orwell's decision was made decades before. It was Orwell's decision but he was conditioned to make a decision.

I said, "But isn't that a contradiction?"

He smiled and said, "Exactly. That's prison. Most people live their lives in absolutes, but not us."

He quoted, "Only intelligent people contradict themselves, motherfucker."

That was Wilde—sort of.

And then, later on, he talked about how his mother crossed rivers to sneak into this country from Mexico—and how he was the child of a black father and a Mexican mother. He talked about how his father was murdered before he was born and how he grew up watching his mother smoke crack. And then he said how this had to have influenced the decisions he later made on the streets. Then one of the guys asked him if his mother was still alive.

He told us he didn't know. But he was counting the days until he got out of here. He only had five years left. He was going to try and find her when he got out and take care of her.

Even though he had been making fun of this just a few minutes before, he was so sincere about it and everyone grew quiet.

So over the next couple of months I got to know the guys better and I kept thinking about Rodriguez. I kept thinking, "I can't believe this guy. I mean most of these prison guys were guys just wanting to get back in here even after they got out. Most of them had the minds of accountants. They were like most of us on the outside— the next score, moving somewhere and changing your life, that sort of thinking. But here was someone who was different. Here was someone whose mind went sideways instead of up and down."

Over the next couple of classes I listened to Rodriguez quote, "Nothing human is alien to me."

One night he made the argument that at the core of every technological innovation was a new mind altering chemical of some kind—whether it be Egyptian, Greek, Roman, Christian, or Silicon Valley even.

I read one of his essays about finding his mother, about his hope of finding her after he got out in five years.

So one night walking out of the prison yard after lockdown, the prison guard Kincaid looked over at me and said, "You don't let them niggers write in Ebonics just like they speak do you?"

I was shocked hearing it.

I didn't know what to say.

I gathered my thoughts, thinking of how to respond, "Well writing is more than spelling."

He said, "Yeah, well these guys are smart. But you can't trust any of them. These guys all made their choices, but they just made bad choices."

But going home that night I wanted to tell him about Rodriguez.

I wanted to tell him about Rodriguez and how beautiful he wrote.

I wanted to tell him how wrong he was.

I wanted to tell him about Rodriguez's murdered father.

And I wanted to tell him about Rodriguez's mother and how he didn't know where she was, but Rodriguez was counting the days until his release.

Five years. Five years.

It wasn't a long time when you really thought about it.

And he was going to try and find her.

But what did it matter?

I figured it was best to encourage Rodriguez because there were just a couple of weeks left of class anyway. So one night I listened to Rodriguez joke with me about it being my birthday and what kind of crazy guy chooses to spend his birthday in prison.

He said, "Well, we should get a stripper for you."

I said, "I don't know about you Rodriguez but it doesn't look to me like you have much access to women in here. I don't know what I'd end up with."

He just laughed and said, "Oh hell McClanahan, you just close your eyes and pretend and it's all the same. I swear to you it's better than on the outside because it all happens between the ears. It *all* happens in the mind."

One night, the day before the last class, I sat in my living room and I told my wife, "I feel like I need to say something to this guy. I know it sounds stupid, but I feel like I need to say something."

I felt like I needed to encourage him somehow, so that when he got out in a couple of years—he really could do this. I needed to tell him when he got out I would help him in any way I could, write to anyone he needed. I thought about all of the stupid shit I've done in my life. Things I've never been punished for, even now.

I went back on the final night of our class and I gave back the essays. I told them it seemed like just a couple of days ago, but three months had already passed. The summer session was over. I shook all of their hands and told them good luck, and they shook my hand and told me good luck. And just as they were leaving, I stopped Rodriguez and I told him how great his essays were, and how he could do this.

I told him how much his stories had meant to me.

I told him he really could find his mother if he wanted.

Five years.

I told him not to let these guys kick the human being out of him.

It was only five years.

And Rodriguez just looked at me like he couldn't believe what I was saying.

He looked at me like I was messing with him.

Then he said, "Oh, I'm not getting out of here McClanahan. I'm a fucking lifer—murder one. I just made all of that shit up for you to have something to talk about in this stupid fucking class."

I didn't know what to say. Was he joking? I couldn't tell with guys in here.

He went out into the yard and started talking to a couple of guys and they started laughing too.

It was stupid, wasn't it? Thesis statements, transitional phrases, topic sentences, 119046, 117843.

I looked at Rodriguez's face and I didn't want it to be true. It was like no matter how long he tried he was never going to be able to teach me anything.

So I thought about his mother—gone.

I thought about his murdered father—gone.

I thought about his hope and his stories—all gone.

And so later that night, waiting for Kincaid to walk me out, Kincaid looked out of the barred glass of education and pointed to

Rodriguez who was standing beneath a flickering light, all alone, smoking a cigarette.

Kincaid, the prison guard, said, "You see that guy there. That guy is smarter than shit—probably the smartest fucking guy in here. He goes around like a fucking gang banger, but the truth is, he's just a spoiled ass rich kid from the suburbs what I hear. Look, doesn't even have any tats on him. Look at his face. His face is smooth. From what I hear he ended up killing somebody."

I stood looking at Rodriguez and I thought about waiting and loving mothers and crossing far away rivers.

I heard Kincaid say, "You can't trust any of these guys. Everybody has a choice in this life. You remember what I told you the first day we met?"

It was like Kincaid wasn't even talking to me anymore, but was repeating a mantra of some kind, a mantra known only to him.

I looked at Rodriguez and wondered who he killed, a girlfriend, a dealer?

His mother?

So that night after lockdown Kincaid gathered up his radio and his prison keys and we made small talk. Then he took out a picture of this little girl and showed it to me. It was a picture of Kincaid's little girl who was about two years old with blonde hair, and she was wearing a hat that had a little cartoon kitten on it.

"She's a beauty isn't she?"

"Yeah she's a cute kid."

"Oh God I love her so much," Kincaid said.

And so Kincaid put it back into his pocket and his face shined so full of love.

I went home that night feeling like I was going to be sick.

I listened in my head as Kincaid's words twirled about how proud he was and how he loved the little girl.

I thought about her face.

Maybe he was right. We all make choices in this world and that was the scary part. Kincaid's little girl was so far away from this place. Kincaid's little girl was so far away from the talk of lockdowns, TB outbreaks, prison riots, drug convictions, and lying men.

So I was surprised a year or two later, after I stopped teaching a class at the federal prison because it was just too much. I awoke one morning and there was snow on the ground. I turned on the television and saw a picture of a little girl on the local television newscast. There was something about the picture of this little girl that looked familiar. She was two years old in the picture and she had blonde hair and she was wearing this hat with a Hello Kitty on it. I felt like I knew this girl. I saw a man being escorted into court wearing an orange jumpsuit and he looked familiar. I saw who it was. I saw who it was before the reporter even said his name, "Kincaid…a prison guard for the past ten years at the federal prison in Beckley."

Then the reporter said Kincaid was being arraigned that morning for the murder of his three-year-old daughter who was found beaten to death the day before.

Now I saw one last thing.

It was the little girl in the picture—gone.

I sat watching the television and I saw Kincaid's sad and shocked face. I thought back to the class and I heard Rodriguez quoting, "Nothing human is alien to me."

I whispered to myself, "Nothing human is alien to me. Nothing human is alien to me."

That was the scary part.

And so I sat and wondered if this is the way the world works. I knew you couldn't trust anyone in this life, not even yourself. I wondered what murder was waiting inside of me to commit. I wondered what murder was waiting inside of the person who was reading this.

And so now I lay me down to sleep and sometimes I dream this strange dream. I dream that we're all back at the federal prison except we're outside the prison walls now. We're all there, all the people I've ever known and all the people in the world are there. And you're there too. We're all cold and scared and shivering and Kincaid and Rodriguez are there as well. They're arguing over this life and what our actions are guided by. No one can figure it out. No one can figure out who the prisoners are and who the prison guards are, and who even the guilty are. And so we're all standing outside the prison walls and we're all arguing over this. It's night. And there's lightning—a black and white night.

And we're all fighting.

We're all fighting to get back inside.

SUICIDE NOTES

It had been a rough year already and I needed someone to talk to.

One morning I was just hanging out in my office and I clicked on an e-mail.

It was from my boss, and it said, *I'm sorry to inform everyone about the passing of our colleague, Nicole Owings, this morning at CAMC in Charleston. More details and funeral arrangements to follow.*

I sat at my desk and felt like somebody had kicked the shit out of me.

Nicole Owings.

She couldn't have been 50.

I guessed it was a heart attack or something.

Then Mr. Davis stuck his head through my door and said, "Did you get the e-mail?" I shook my head yes.

He said, "Isn't that horrible? I guess it must have been a heart attack or something."

I went down to the main office and asked the secretary, "What happened?"

She put her hand over her mouth and whispered, "She shot herself."

Then the phone rang and she repeated the same thing to the person on the other line. "She shot herself."

I walked back down the long hallway towards my office and I just sat there alone. I didn't even do anything but just kept thinking about how I saw her just a couple of days before. Nicole was always the type of person who looked you in the eye when she shook your hand and said, "You having a good day?"

She was always the type of person who meant it.

She was always the type of person who said, "Thanks for helping me out and doing such a good job."

She wasn't like most people at work who just bitch-bitch-bitch and then bitch some more.

That afternoon I cried in my office and left a little early telling the secretary on my way out the door, "You just don't know people do you?"

She shook her head and said, "Yeah, you just don't know people."

She'd been crying too.

Over the next couple of days, I started putting together all of the details. I heard from one person who said she was unhappy with her job. Then I heard from another person that she'd bought a weapon recently. It all started rolling together. Someone said the police had yet to rule out murder because the gunshot wound was in her chest. Then the guy down the hall said maybe our bosses had her killed. He was always spinning crazy conspiracy theories about the bosses.

I thought, "Just because they didn't give you a raise last year doesn't mean they're murderers. Not everything in the world has to do with you not getting a raise you fucking asshole."

The next thing I heard was this. The gunshot wound wasn't in the chest. She shot herself in the neck. Someone said it was incredibly unusual for a woman to commit suicide by shooting herself, rather than taking pills.

I tried asking people why would someone want to shoot herself in the neck.

I went through all of the scenarios I could think of.

#1. She was nervous and the gun slipped.

#2. She was in such pain that she didn't know what she was doing.

#3. Maybe she regretted it at the last second and tried to pull away, but it was too late.

Then finally I came up with this one, "No, she was a good Baptist. She wanted her family to be able to wake her with an open casket."

Sarah looked at me and said, "Why do you keep thinking about it?"

I couldn't stop thinking about it. I looked through the paper for her obituary and there was only a short one. There wasn't even going to be a memorial service, and like most things you forget about them.

So here it was another Thursday, and I was sitting at my desk when I heard a knock at the door. It was a woman I knew whose husband had died a couple of months earlier from a heart problem at the age of twenty-eight. Before it happened, they were having marriage problems, so he went to Florida to stay with his father. His father said he went to bed early one night and the next morning when the father went to wake the kid up, the kid was just dead.

And now here she was not two months later and she still looked shocked.

She said, "I hate to bother you Scott, but do you have a second? I know you have a lot of stuff going on."

I turned around and even though I didn't want to—I said, "Yeah what's going on? What do you need?"

She sat down at one of the chairs in front of my desk and there were tears in her eyes.

She said, "You know how my husband died a while back?"

I nodded my head at the young widow and said, "Yeah, it's horrible. How are you?"

She just lowered her head and said, "Well that's what I came to talk to you about."

And then her face twisted and turned into all kinds of fucked up shapes.

Uh-oh.

She took a deep breath and said, "Well you know how his father told me it was a heart problem?"

I nodded my head yes. She told me that the autopsy came back and it wasn't a heart problem. She told me the autopsy came back and said something else.

It came back and said, Manner of Death: suicide.

I got up from my desk and went over and patted her on the back.

O Jamie.

O Jamie.

And then she reached into her purse and showed me what she had been given the day before by her father-in-law. It was a note her husband wrote before he took a whole bottle full of pills. It was a note that said,

I've had a good life. But I'm not doing any good. Tell my wife I love her. Please don't feel sorry. But remember all of the good times. I'm going away now. Love, Jesse.

So I kept patting her on the back like I was burping a baby.

I patted her again and again and said, "Well have you talked to anyone about it?"

She cried and shook her head, "No."

I said, "Well I know Mr. Golden is somebody who is really good to talk with here at work."

Mr. Golden.

He was this older man who always seemed so strong. He was someone you could talk to and who always made sense. He was someone who had answers and not just bullshit answers—there's a reason for everything, that kind of shit, but answers you could believe. He was somebody who helped me when I was having it rough. And so I told Jamie she should go and talk to him. I told her Mr. Golden could help.

That evening I went home and just felt like shit. I thought, "What a shitty couple of weeks." I turned the television on and watched this show about, yep, suicide.

"Good God," I said and turned the channel. But I couldn't stop thinking about it. I turned it back and watched. I watched how in families once a suicide happens, the rest of the family is more likely to commit suicide. Then I thought about my own grandfather's family. There were eleven of them and five committed suicide. At first it was the father, and then two years later a daughter, and then a year after that another daughter, and then a son, and then another son.

It was like a fever almost. It was like a fever of some kind that you could catch and once you caught it—you couldn't do anything about it. I started telling Sarah, "We like to think of ourselves as complicated. But we're not. The whole world is just a virus."

That night I called my mother on the phone and I told her all about what was going on. I told her about how much things had been bothering me. I told her it had been a rough year and I couldn't stop thinking about it.

My mom just said, "Well maybe you should go and talk to someone Scott. There's been a lot of bad stuff happening. Maybe you should go and talk to someone and it'll make you feel better."

So I decided to go and talk to Golden. I decided to go and talk to Mr. Golden and tell him what was bothering me. I wanted to tell him how it seemed like every Thursday something bad was happening, and that's just what I did.

I knocked on his door and I said, "Dean, I'm sorry to bother you. But I was just wondering if I could talk to you for a few minutes?"

He turned around at his desk and said just like I always said, "Yeah sure, what's going on?"

I started, "Well this stuff with Nicole has really been bothering me."

And as soon as I said it his face looked all different.

He leaned over and his voice started cracking and popping, "You know I was the last one to talk to her before she went home."

He said, "And I didn't even realize, but the last thing she said to me was, 'I wish you the best of luck.'"

He said he didn't even know what that meant at the time. He didn't realize.

So I tried telling him something else to make myself feel better. I needed to talk about it. I tried to interrupt him and get it off my chest. But his hands were shaking now and he was crying, "You know she shot herself that evening and they didn't even find her until the next morning."

He said, "I just keep thinking of her alone there all night. I just can't get it off my mind."

I said, "Well it's really been..."

But then I stopped, and I knew he couldn't help me.

He bent over and put his head in his hands. He started rocking back and forth and saying over and over, "But I won't do it. I won't do it. I have too much to live for. I have my son. I have my son. I can't leave him."

I walked over and patted him on the back.

I whispered, "Now don't you talk like that."

He looked at me and I saw he didn't have any answers. He couldn't solve anything. He tried to reassure me, "Don't worry Scott. I'm not going to do it."

And then he said in another voice, "I'm going to do it. I'm going to do it."

And then he started laughing a laugh that wasn't even a laugh but a cackle.

He kept rocking and saying, "I'm not going to do it. I'm going to do it. I mean I'm not."

So I just slowly started backing away. He kept laughing. And so I left. I walked out of his office and kept on walking. It was a fever. It was a fever, and I didn't want to catch it.

It was a fever I prayed wasn't inside me at that very moment.

So I got in my car and went home. That night I tried to keep my mind off of it by checking my e-mail. There was only one—an old e-mail from a friend of mine. It said, *Would you please give me a call? Danny and I broke up this morning. He told me we should get different places. I'm feeling really down. Please give me a call. Please. And if I don't hear from you Scott—*

And then she wrote these words...

I wish you the best of luck.

And so I thought about these last words I'd heard before.

I knew these words. They were Nicole's last words.

"I wish you the best of luck."

So I didn't call. I turned off the computer and I didn't call because I'd caught the fever. I took down a sheet of paper and I started writing down what happened. And now at the end of writing this—I find that it's not an account I've been writing, but a note of some kind. This fever can be passed through a story too.

I find myself writing a note that you'll be writing soon. It's a note that ends like this,

I've lived a good life. But I'm no good at it. Tell my wife I love her. Tell her to remember the happy times. I'm going away now. Love, Scott.

FABLE #1

My mom had been teaching for thirty-three years and it was starting to get to her.

It used to be she came in all smiling and happy and telling funny stories. Now it was different. She was worn down and tired. One day she walked in through the door carrying her school books with this tired look on her face.

She sat down in the la-z-boy and said, "I had the strangest thing happen to me today. It's something I've never seen in all my years."

She sat in the la-z-boy and told us about a little boy who had it rough at home.

She told us about how her class had just come back from music and they were sitting in their desks talking. She noticed this little boy doing something at his desk.

She watched him for a few minutes and then she went back to his desk and said, "What are you doing R.J.? What are you doing with that chalk dust?"

There was chalk dust on his nose and he had a rolled up piece of paper he was snorting it with.

R.J. looked up with his 4th grade eyes and said, "I'm taking my medicine like mom."

My mom said she didn't even say anything to him. She went back to her desk and sat down.

I saw my mother's eyes fill full of tears, and I thought to myself that this was my mother. This was the woman who had taught children how to add and divide.

That night after the little boy snorted the chalk dust and she came home with tears in her eyes, I sat down and tried talking with her.

She sat in her chair and said, "I guess I'm just a failure."

I said, "Oh Mom. It's not that. Do you think that maybe you're just kind of burnt out?"

She thought about it for awhile and then she said, "I don't think it's that. I just think these kids have changed. This is a different place now."

I knew all about it. There were 100,000 coal jobs in West Virginia in 1950 and now there were 15,000. 75% of the kids were either on free or reduced lunch. I told her this but it didn't help.

She started crying and said, "I guess I'm just a failure."

I knew I had to do something. I went over to the counter and picked up dad's calculator and I said, "But think about all the kids you've taught. I mean think about it, somehow you've made a difference."

I punched into the calculator the number 33.

I said, "You've taught thirty-three years."

I added those three years she would have taught if she hadn't stayed home with me. I took an average class size of twenty-five students and then I multiplied that together. Then I hit the equal key. The total was close to one thousand students.

I showed it to her and I said, "Look at this. You've taught 1,000 kids."

She held the calculator and looked at the number 1,000. She pushed the tears away from her eyes and sniffed a sniff.

She smiled a tiny smile and said, "I know I had one student Steve Meadows and he's a doctor now."

Of course, I'd been hearing about Steven since I was a little boy. I'd been hearing about Steven graduating valedictorian from high school and leading the small high school to their first state football championship in fifty years.

And like now the story always ended with, "And you know what? I think he's a doctor now."

I remembered being a little boy and watching my mother cut out his senior picture from the newspaper after he'd won a scholarship. I remembered listening to the radio when Meadow Bridge High School held Pineville on the goal line in the Class A state championship.

4th and 2.

Pineville with the ball.

The snap—the quarterback rolls right.

He throws.

The receiver bobbles the throw and it's knocked away.

It's a miracle.

They stop them.

We sat at home and cheered and my mother said, "You know I was the one who taught that little boy to read, and he was such a good student. He caught on so quick."

It wasn't a week later my dad came home and said, "Did you hear Sheridan died? The obituary is in the paper."

He started looking through the paper.

My mother said, "Oh that's too bad."

This was Steven's grandfather.

"I guess I should go then," she said.

So she did. She went to the wake of her favorite student's grandfather. Of course, she hadn't even seen this student since he was in the first grade. She stood in the back because it was so packed. Then she saw Steven's mother. Steven's mother waved. And my mom waved.

My mom asked, "And how's Steven?"

"Oh he should be here any second. He's brought in the wife and the kids. He's so busy."

My mother said, "Yeah I know I'm getting ready to retire next year and it makes you feel good when one of your students succeeds. It makes you feel worthwhile."

This guy walked in with these three kids behind him. There was a tired looking woman too with a baby in her arms and a huge diaper bag across her shoulder. Immediately the three children started running around knocking things over.

Steven's mother said, "Oh there's Steven. Steven, come here."

Steven walked over.

Steven's mother said, "Steven. Do you know who this is?"

Steven was all sweaty and chubby. He wasn't like the high school football hero or the valedictorian, or the cute little first grader.

He looked at his mom with this disgusted look on his face and said, "Now mom how am I supposed to know every person you introduce me to?"

Steven's mother slapped his shoulder like he was being rude, "Don't you remember Mrs. McClanahan? She was your first grade teacher."

Steven looked at Mom like she was a stranger and then he shook his head, "NOOOO! I don't remember. That was a long time ago. I don't know who she is."

Mrs. Meadows slapped his arm again and then Steven walked away.

My mother taught for thirty-three years and Steven Meadows didn't know who she was.

FABLE #2

My dad worked at Kroger for thirty-three years and he used to come home every day at 3:30 and tell me what happened. There was a mentally retarded man, Rex, who used to stand outside Kroger, day after day, and sell Grit newspapers. The Grit was a paper full of stories like...

HOW I GREW PRIZEWINNING SQUASH IN MY GARDEN THIS YEAR...

...10 EASY STEPS TO LOSE WEIGHT AND EAT ALL THE BREAD YOU WANT...

...BARBARA MANDRELL, THE SECRETS OF MY SUCCESS. And each day when my father took his break, Rex walked right up to him, just like he did the day before and asked him, "@#$*?"

My dad said, "What?"

Rex adjusted his fur coat and his big thick glasses and said, "Know what time it is?"

My dad looked at his watch and said, "Yeah it's 10:15."

Rex said, "Wanna @#$%^?"

My dad said, "What?"

Rex said, "You want to buy a newspaper?"

It was like this every day. My dad took his break at 10:15.

Rex shuffled over in his giant winter coat even though it was the middle of summer, "You know what time it is?"

My dad looked at his watch and said, "10:15."

Rex swung the yellow bag he kept the papers in and said, "You want to buy a paper?"

My dad said, "No."

Sometimes my dad got there early enough to see Rex's eighty-year-old mother drop him off in front of Kroger and say, "Now you have a good day Rex."

Rex said, "OK Mom."

Every day Rex stood out front and sold maybe two or three papers. I remember being a little boy and being afraid of him. I was afraid of the others who gathered in front of the stores too. I remember being afraid of the man with cerebral palsy who if you dropped a quarter in his bucket, he gave you a brand new pencil. He could hardly move, but he just sat there all day asking for money.

Then one afternoon my dad talked about how Rex had been selling those papers for years and how he heard Rex's mother was having trouble seeing. She couldn't drive anymore.

He said, "I don't know what Rex is going to do when his mother is gone."

The next day it was more of the same.

The next day it was Rex saying, "You know what time it is Mack?"

And then, "You wanna buy a paper?"

My dad said, "No I don't wanna buy a paper."

Every day it was like this. Every day it was throwing around fifty pound bags of potatoes and watching this old couple come in shouting at each other.

The old woman always led the old man, shouting at him, "You crazy asshole."

The old man shouted, "That's right I'm a crazy motherfucker. I was crazy enough to marry you—you old bitch."

The old man went off one way and the old woman turned to my dad, "Now how much are these green beans, honey?"

My dad pointed to the price and she shook her head and said, "Oh gracious. I can't afford that. I'm just a little old lady on a fixed income."

My dad turned his back to her and he looked up into the mirror above and saw the old woman open her purse and put the greens in because if there's something an old woman loves to do—it's shoplift. Then she pushed her buggy down the aisle like it was nothing.

He didn't say anything because he had other things to worry about. The order was in. The order was a couple of tons of fresh produce fresh off the truck.

"What are we doing standing around? Let's start putting this away," my dad said.

And so they did, but they started doing it all wrong. They had the strawberries over here and the cucumbers over there. The giant freezer they kept it all in wasn't rotated right so he came in and chewed some ass. "Old stuff has to go out on the racks and in front. New stuff in the back. It's called rotation."

This was the way it was every day. It was my father getting up before the sun rose and going to work, and then the next day getting up, looking into my door and going to work. Then the next day it was getting up and going to work, and coming home at 3:30.

The next day it was just the same. It was two hours of moving watermelons, and my father's arms so tired he could hardly lift them. His polio legs were already starting to ache. An hour later it was the old woman yelling at her husband. She called him crazy and a bastard, and he called her wore out and an old bitch, and how she was crazier than shit. This went back and forth, back and forth, until the sweet little old lady turned to my dad just like always and said, "Now how much for a mess of these string beans?"

My dad told her.

She turned to him with her scrunched up face and said, "Oh gosh—that's too expensive. I'm just a little old lady on a fixed income."

My father turned and walked away and watched her in the mirror. She opened up her purse and put the string beans in.

My father turned back to her and said, "Mam. I'm sorry but I just saw you put those string beans in your purse."

She smiled and looked at him. She opened up her purse and put them back, saying, "Oh gosh. You caught me."

Then she walked on down the aisle to keep shoplifting other things like microwave popcorn.

Dad went outside to take his break and it didn't get any better. He sat drinking his pop and watching his watch for the fifteen minutes to end. Rex walked towards him all sweaty without any teeth and wearing his pop bottle thick glasses.

He was saying, "Buh buh buh" which meant, "You know what time it is Mack?"

This had been going on for years though and my Dad had had enough. He couldn't take it anymore.

My dad said, "Rex, why don't you tell me what time it is?"

Rex looked at my dad's watch. It said 10:15.

Rex looked down at it and said, "It says 10:15, Mack."

And then Rex smiled a smile because he knew what time it was.

He'd been doing this for years and he always knew what time it was.

He needed someone to talk to.

THE FUTURE TELLER

I've always had the gift. Ever since I was a little boy I could see into the future, or at least I could tell when something bad was going to happen. It used to come to me in my dreams or it would just be a feeling. I got it from my grandma Ruby. She was always seeing into the future or finding out what would happen to the world through her dreams.

Every time I left her house she said, "Oh Lordie Todd, don't you get killed in a car accident on them roads."

I told her just like always, "Grandma, my name is not Todd. My name is Scott, but I'll be careful."

I guess if you have thirteen children like she did, grandchildren, great grandchildren, friends, neighbors, secret enemies, and every one of them gets ready to leave and you tell them to be careful because they might be killed, at least one or two of them are bound to find tragedy along the way.

I don't know if that's what you call future telling or not.

I knew I had the gift when I was about eight years old and awoke from a dream about my uncle Charlie. My uncle built houses. He actually drank beer and smoked cigarettes while someone paid him to build houses, but if you asked me what he did—that's what I'd tell you. In my dream we were going to his funeral except his funeral wasn't a funeral really. My aunt Mandy was crying and my grandma Ruby was crying, and all of my cousins were crying, and my uncle Charlie was there, all rotten and dark looking. He wasn't even saying, "sheeeeeeeeeeeeeeeeeettttt," which was his catchphrase, the longest drawn out "sheeeeeeeeeeeeeettttt" you've ever heard in your life. He was quiet now.

I woke up from this dream about Uncle Charlie and went into the kitchen and told my mother about it.

I told my mother that my uncle died in my dream.

My mother said, "Oh Scott, don't worry about it, it's just a dream."

I thought this was a pretty silly thing to say to a future teller. But it wasn't three hours later my grandma Ruby called and said my Uncle Charlie was in an accident. He was working a circular saw and cut his thumb off.

They reattached it.

That evening I asked my mom if she thought it meant anything, my dream about my uncle Charlie.

My mom said, "Well you know, you've always kind of been like that. I know your grandma Ruby is always seeing things in her dreams."

Then she told me about how her uncle James died when he was just twelve years old.

A bird flew in the house the day before, and if you're a country person and a bird flies into your house, you better get ready because some shit is going to go down.

Of course, my dad didn't think there was anything to the dream though.

He said, "Getting a thumb cut off is a lot different than dying boy. Besides that, they reattached the thumb so it's not like he even had his thumb cut off in the first place."

He didn't think I had the future seeing gift.

But I knew I did. I knew I did one night when I dreamed about being trapped at the Rainelle sporting goods store with all of these black bears. Unfortunately, the next day I had to go to the Rainelle sporting goods store and take a movie back. It was a sporting goods store, but like most local businesses they had about three different things inside. For example, you could rent a movie, buy a thirty-thirty rifle, get your twelve point stuffed by a taxidermist or even get a tan in the tanning bed if you needed one bad enough (NEW BULBS!). I knew my dream about black bears wasn't a good sign, but I needed to take the movie back.

As soon as I went inside, I knew I should have trusted my dream. I smelled this weird smell in the place. My neighbor Bobbie B. was working there. He was about twenty. And there was this new kid who was working there too. He was only about eighteen.

Of course, my dad always told me again and again when I was a kid, "I never want you shooting guns with Bobbie B."

He saw Bobbie B. coming out of the woods one day and didn't approve of the way he was holding his firearm or something. So I was real careful around Bobbie B. at the sporting goods store.

I turned the movie back in, but as soon as I did, I felt this horrible feeling.

The new kid handed me back the change, except when he did, it all fell out of his hand and landed on the counter and then the floor, clinging and clanging all around us. It kept bouncing around and the new kid bent down on one knee and started picking it up. He looked up at me and started saying over and over again, "I'm so sorry. I'm so sorry." And it wasn't like he was saying those stupid sayings we always say just to have something to say. How are you? I'm fine. How are you? Oh I'm sorry, etc.

It was like he was confessing something to me. It was like he was confessing something to me about his own life, like he was looking for help.

I kept whispering inside my head. "Something bad is going to happen here. Something bad is going to happen here. I need to leave."

And when I looked up, guess what I saw?

I saw a stuffed black bear tied up beside all of the other taxidermy animals.

And you know what?

The black bear was staring at me.

I just left. I clamped my change into my twisted fist, and I started walking towards the door, past the new kid who whispered sorry one last time, past Bobbie B., who waved at me, past Ulysses Phipps who everyone called "useless."

"Hey McClanahan," Ulysses said, walking through the door. I just kept right on walking.

I didn't know what was happening.

I didn't know a lot of things.

I didn't know Ulysses had been saving his money so he could buy a .44 Magnum.

I didn't know he was obsessed with buying one of the most powerful handguns the world had to offer.

I didn't know anything about it, but I could feel something was wrong, so I just let the door slam behind me.

I tried not thinking about it. When I was driving away I saw Bobbie B. come running outside. He was crying and he was covered in blood. He threw himself against the hood of his truck.

A couple of seconds later an ambulance came ripping into the parking lot. The Quinwood Volunteer ambulance never came zipping anywhere. It was the type of ambulance where you needed to check your pockets after they dropped you off.

So I just left.

Later that day my dad called and said, "Did you hear Bobbie killed a boy? I told you to be careful around him."

"Who?" I said.

"That boy he worked with—that new kid who was working there."

"What?"

"He ended up shooting him. That's what they're saying anyway."

And so over the next couple of days I started putting together the story from a couple of different people. One person said Ulysses had come in to buy a .44 and he did. I knew that. Bobbie and the new kid sold it to him.

The new kid bent down over the counter and started filling out the license. Bobbie didn't know it was loaded, and started messing with the trigger. It was either that or he thought it was a blank.

Another person said no one really knew. The gun fired. Bobbie B. shot the new kid. The bullet hit the kid in the neck, and then down, ricocheted off his collar bone and busted back up into his skull, before blowing the top of the new kid's head off.

The new kid dropped to the ground.

Boom.

Bobbie B. freaked.

Ulysses left.

And then somebody else told me that Bobbie B. fell to his knees and started doing CPR. It was just like on television.

He started doing CPR like a crazy man, even though the top of the kid's head was gone.

He just kept right on doing it, even though every time he did— blood shot out of the top of the kid's head like a water fountain flowing red.

One one thousand.
BLOOD.
Two one thousand.
BLOOD.
He kept doing CPR until the cops came and pulled him off.

That evening Bobbie B. went home and tried to hang himself behind the locked door of his bedroom.

It didn't work.

So after it was all over I wondered whether I could really see into the future or not. I looked through the Bible about people seeing visions in dreams and then interpreting those dreams. I thought that maybe I couldn't see into the future and that I only connected things later.

This is how things usually work, right?

Some shit happens and then someone says I knew about it all along. I asked my mother and sometimes she laughed. But then sometimes she didn't.

I asked my father and he always just shook his head "No."

So I wondered.

I wondered about my grandma Ruby and her dreams. I wondered about the feeling I had in the Rainelle sporting goods store that day.

I started asking myself, was it true? Could I really see into the future?

So I ask you now—would you tell me I was wrong? Would you tell me I was wrong if I said I had a dream about you last night? And in this dream I saw into your future. I saw you living a long and happy life. In this dream I saw you walking out the door tomorrow and finding true love, if you haven't already. I saw your children growing healthy and strong and throwing their arms around you saying, "I love you Mommy. I love you Daddy. I love you forever." I saw you living there in this future world without pain, surrounded by children and grandchildren and great-grandchildren, and knowing one thing in this world, knowing that you will never grow old, and knowing that you will never die.

So I ask you now.

Would you tell me I am wrong?

THE COAL TRAIN SOUNDS #1

So sometimes at night I just sat up in my bed and listened to all the mountain sounds. I'd leave a little night light on and listen to radio stations snapping and popping from as far away as New York or Atlanta. And sometimes I sat up with a candle light reading books by writers whose names I didn't even know how to pronounce. So right before sleep I might shut my eyes and listen to the dogs barking outside—far away dogs, barking so loud like a ghost was walking among them.

Sometimes I wished I was one of these dogs and sometimes I wished that ghost was me. And then at 11:30 the coal train came blowing through town just like every night. I listened as it blew and whistled and whispered. I imagined that coal train going somewhere just as I imagine it now, to Norfolk or the north. And then afterwards—Japan.

THE END

So this is the end of the book. You should throw it in the trash and get up.

Quit checking your Goddamn e-mail so much. Flush that cell phone down the toilet. There's a whole world outside. Let's break into blossom.

COAL TRAIN SOUNDS #2

And if I'm far away and gone and you want to find me, go to Rainelle, WV on any given night. The street will be empty at 11:30. So go there and listen for it and I'll come running. We'll ride where the black train takes us, deep into the mountains, deep into a place where no one knows our name, like our very own time machine, taking us not far into the future, but deep into the past, before any of the towns were here, before we were even born. We'll be dinosaurs then and at last we won't even exist. Thank God.

And so now you're saying, "What's that sound?"

I say, "That's the sound of the coal train coming. It's coming to take us away."

ARE YOU READY?

AMERICAN GENIUS

An Afterword by Sam Pink

Scott McClanahan is from West Virginia, which, as he has to explain to another person in STORIES II, is not just a part of Virginia, but an entire state of its own. It is at this point in my reading of Scott's work that I resolved to kill him if I ever met him. To put my hands on his throat and choke him to death as he stares, confused, into my emotionless face. No, actually I never thought that about Scott. I've never thought about killing him until I wrote that sentence. Then, when I wrote that sentence, I went off into a staring fantasy where I kind of envisioned it up until the moment he dies. Shit, now that I wrote that, I actually imagined him dying. And you know what, I'm a lot sadder than I thought I'd be, having fantasized in vivid detail about choking tens, nay, hundreds of dozens of people, both faceless and recognizable.

Anyway, Scott wears suits from Sears. He came to Chicago a couple summers ago and we read together and we drank beer out of a glass boot at this German restaurant. We saw German Larry Bird play in a polka band. Scott also showed me his impression of a person laughing while typing a mean comment on the internet. These are things we shared during our first encounter. It was at that point in our meeting that I resolved to live in a glass boot with him—if we ever both needed a place to live and/or had access to a shrink ray.

But that was only the first time we met. The next couple of years saw us drinking forty ouncers in different alleys throughout Chicago, preparing ourselves to read our work to audiences. Scott is really nice, and I'll say this: he is really good at keeping up the whole "I'm actually from West Virginia" bit. I mean, he does the accent, he affects that "hillbilly politeness" that everyone seems so fond of, and most importantly, he wears suits from Sears.

All of this, plus how much I liked his first book, STORIES, and his new book, STORIES II, has solidified Scott McClanahan as a friend and as an author who I will continue to read. He writes un-selfconsciously minimalist stories about people from West Virginia. Both collections in this collection, STORIES and STORIES II, were originally published by Six Gallery Press, a small press in Pittsburgh. I am glad Cameron Pierce is now in control of these books. So glad, that I am now going to vividly imagine choking Cameron's body into lifelessness.

STORIES was originally given to me by Barry Graham. He told me I'd like it. He handed it to me and I liked the cover. Then I read the whole thing on a bus from Ann Arbor back to Chicago. I sat there quietly reading it, but inside my head I kept putting my hand up to my mouth and going "ohhhhh" like someone does after they see someone get brutally dunked on in basketball. I was a fan of his work immediately. I pretty much dislike everything I read, but I liked Scott's work right away. Somehow after that we emailed each other and started doing readings together.

STORIES II followed soon after.

STORIES II returns to the themes of STORIES: West virginia, being a person around other people, and figuring things out when you thought they were already figured out.

STORIES II also returns to the signature tone of STORIES. He writes in a way that is conscious of both his own absurdity and that of others, without overdoing either. He makes it really easy to like the narrator and to learn from the narrator's experiences. Scott also knows how to balance humor and sadness.

Scott's style is the most lively minimalism I have read. Many sentences begin with "and" or "so" and contain the word "just." The result is a really smooth minimalism. Not a minimalism that recognizes itself, but one that just happens. If you are ever able to see Scott read, you will understand what I mean. Many of his stories begin as though you just walked up to a conversation. Not "in the middle of things" but "in the middle of thoughts." For example, one story begins, "I've stolen things before though." The result is that it's like you are put into an already-begun conversation.

I don't know what else to say. I called off work today and I'm drinking alcohol. I don't really drink alcohol that much. I'm sitting on a wood floor. I'm wearing these shorts I just bought from a

Salvation Army. I already spilled fucking cocktail sauce on them. I don't know. I mean, look at how the tone changes from the first half to the second. Maybe I'm not the same person anymore. I think Scott recently became a father. Which is pretty sweet I guess. Anyway, thanks for buying/reading this book. I support it fully. And I really don't care about much. But Scott is an author of American Genius.

April 4, 2012
Chicago, Illinois.

ABOUT THE AUTHOR

Scott McClanahan is the author of *Stories V!* (Holler Presents, 2011), *Crapalachia* (Two Dollar Radio, 2013), and *Hill William* (Tyrant Books, 2013). He lives in West Virginia.

LAZY FASCIST PRESS

PERSON BY SAM PINK

"If you read just one book this year, let it be Sam Pink's *Person*."
—**Electric Literature**

"It made me laugh and my hair stand on end."
—**HTML Giant**

"Sam Pink is dictator of the island of the bizarre."
—**As You Recognize Your Transience**

BROKEN PIANO FOR PRESIDENT BY PATRICK WENSINK

"Like Christopher Moore on very strong acid. In *Broken Piano For President*, he's created a Pynchonesque universe...A rollicking good time of a novel."
—**Greg Olear**, author of *Fathermucker*

"Not only continues to break fresh Wensinkian ground, he continues to find his voice, a warped voice surely, but one uniquely his own."
—**Ben Tanzer**, author of *You Can Make Him Like You*

ANATOMY COURSES BY BLAKE BUTLER AND SEAN KILPATRICK

"Mined from the same vein as the cut-up experiments of Acker, Burroughs, and Gysin, *Anatomy Courses* is an intoxicating word salad drenched in cloacal dressing. Under layers of scintillating glossolalia, brand-name invocations, ethnic epithets, anatomic cornerstones, and alien parental angst, the careful reader will find a poetic cycle of bawdy body horror."
—**Ross E. Lockhart**, author of *Chick Bassist*

ZOMBIE BAKE-OFF BY STEPHEN GRAHAM JONES

"Jones doesn't pull any punches when it comes to describing the zombies' relentless pursuit. He describes it with gusto and an obvious love for this bloody branch of literature. It's more than mindless fun because Terry and Xombie are smart people with a problem to solve."
—**The Denver Post**

THE DEVIL IN KANSAS BY DAVID OHLE

"No amount of description will prepare you for the icky, cavernous, taboo places in your mind to which he'll lead you, hand in hand, Virgil to your Dante. You'll recognize some of these places, of course. The question is, how did he get in there?"
—**The Believer**

THE OBESE BY NICK ANTOSCA

"Above all, *The Obese* is a satire. It's gory and makes no apologies about it. Writing about body image and America's obesity epidemic, Antosca, a Shirley Jackson Award-winner and author of Midnight Picnic and Fires, takes no prisoners, leaving every man, woman, and child to fend for themselves [. . . .] Living up to his reputation for innovative yet accessible work, Antosca creates a story that is so grotesquely hilarious it makes me wonder if it's, indeed, possible."
—**JMWW**

OF THIMBLE AND THREAT: THE LIFE OF A RIPPER VICTIM BY ALAN M. CLARK

"*Of Thimble and Threat* is a terrifically absorbing read. A mature novel and superbly researched. The image of silver in the blood was woven expertly and made the ending luminous and poignant."
—**Simon Clark**, author of *The Night of the Triffids*

NO ONE CAN DO ANYTHING WORSE TO YOU THAN YOU CAN BY SAM PINK

"Hilarious and black-as-fuck."
—**VICE**

"Wildly imaginative and very entertaining. The author is simply someone who fans of literature must read and this book is just one more step in the ladder that's currently taking Lazy Fascist Press into a place within the publishing industry where there's a lot of room simply because very few have gotten there. Go buy this right now."
—**Horror Talk**

Lightning Source UK Ltd.
Milton Keynes UK
UKOW042356160113

204983UK00003B/393/P